Ink's Second Chance

Infernal Sons MC #6

Carol Dawn

Ink's Second Chance

All rights reserved. This book or any portion thereof may not be reproduced or used without the express written permission of the publisher except for the use of brief quotations in a book review.

Copyright © 2021 Carolyn Jacobs
(Carol Dawn)
All rights reserved

Published by Carolyn Jacobs
Cover by Carolyn Jacobs

Any references to historical events, real people, or real places are used fictitiously. Names, characters, and places are products of the author's imagination.

Dedication

To those who think love won't find you because you're different.
You're perfect just the way you are.
This is for you.

PROLOGUE
Ink

I roll my eyes as I watch Bear, Chains, Hawk, Trigger, and Brick with their partners. They're all laughing and flirting, and it's so fucking domestic I could puke.

I will never understand why men let their dicks get tied down. Being with the same person every single day for the rest of my life does not sound like my kind of fun. I get bored way too quickly.

Women are like candy. Each pussy is flavored just slightly different. Each pussy feels slightly different. Each mouth sucks slightly different. Why in the hell would someone give all of that up?

Not to mention the little monsters. We've turned into a domesticated biker club that serves as a daycare. I fucking hate it.

Okay, maybe *hate* is the wrong word, but I honestly can't understand it.

That being said, I really do love everyone here. I may not understand how these men let their partners chain down their dicks, but I have come to think of them as family. I would do anything for them. I would kill for them, and I would die for them.

"What are you thinking about, brother?" Wolf asks.

Wolf is another man I don't understand. I've known

him for about six months now, and I have never seen him with a woman. Or a man.

"Romance," I admit. "I don't understand it."

"I see," he says. "I think romance is quite beautiful."

"Not you, too," I groan, causing Wolf to laugh.

"Unfortunately, no, not yet," he says. "I haven't found my soulmate yet."

"Soulmate, huh? You are a romantic."

I stand and pat Wolf on the shoulder.

"I'm out, brother," I say, tossing my beer can in the trash. "I need to find a distraction."

"Those *distractions* are going to cause you a great deal of pain one day," Wolf says.

"Yeah, yeah."

It's not the first time I've heard that, and I'm sure it won't be the last. The guys are always telling me that my dick will get me in trouble when I find a special someone. Well, I have news for them. I'll never allow myself to be trapped by a woman.

My dick is free to fuck who I want, and there isn't a single woman alive who can make me rethink my ways.

CHAPTER ONE
Rachal

I think I'm finally going to do it. After a whole year of debating the pros and cons, I've finally made up my mind.

I'm getting a tattoo.

With determination, I call for a taxi and ask him to drop me off at the most popular tattoo shop in my town. There are so many here that I would never be able to choose.

"That would be Ink's Tattoos," the driver says. "He's the best artist in the next three states combined."

Ink's tattoos? Why does that name sound so familiar?

"Thank you," I tell the driver, distractedly.

I know I've heard of that name before. I mean, it's not like it's a common one. But it sure is familiar.

"Here you are, miss," the driver says, coming to a stop. "Do you need any help?"

"Would you mind getting my chair from the trunk?" I ask. "Just open it and bring it by my door, and I can handle the rest."

Did I mention that I'm paralyzed? Because I am.

It happened on my twenty-first birthday. I was out celebrating with my older sister and we were hit by a semi-truck. Amazingly, everyone survived.

The truck driver was arguing with his wife over the

phone and not paying attention to the road. He looked up at the last second and attempted to move the rig back onto his lane.

Unfortunately, he wasn't fast enough, and the tail end of the eighteen-wheeled trailer smashed right into the front end of my car.

My sister, Becky, and the truck driver managed to escape without much injury. Unfortunately, I didn't have that same luck. I wasn't wearing my seatbelt and the force of the impact had jerked my body forward. I was microseconds from flying out of my windshield when the airbag popped out and smashed me back against my seat.

I'm not sure if it was the being jerked forward or the airbag slamming me back, but something had caused irreparable damage to my spinal cord.

Luckily though, I can still feel my legs. Which means I can still feel when I need to use the restroom. I've also been told that I can still have a wonderful sex life. I'll be able to feel everything but won't be able to do all the fun position switches.

Not that it matters anyway. I've made a promise to myself to not settle for anything less than amazing when it comes to a man. I've seen my sister heartbroken over more than one asshole and I don't plan on the same thing happening to me. Well, again.

That accident happened eight years ago. And while it made me lose the mobility in my legs, it also opened my eyes to how the world views people who are different.

I'm not the most beautiful woman in the world, but I think I'm alright. Boy's used to show interest towards me. But now, all I see are looks of pity.

Well, screw them. I don't want their pity. I'm happy

with my life. Sure, it's hard sometimes, but I get by just fine.

After sliding into my chair, I pay and tip the driver before heading towards the small shop that says, Ink's, overtop the door.

I look around and sigh when I see no wheelchair-accessible area. Just steps to reach the sidewalk.

It doesn't matter, though. This isn't the first time I've had to deal with incompetent store owners and their need to save a few bucks. I'll complain later.

I go down the road a little until I see a road sign near the sidewalk. I grab the sign with one of my hands and my wheel with the other. With a little maneuvering and a curse word or two, I've finally made it up on the sidewalk.

I roll myself back toward the shop, open the door, and head inside.

There are images of tattoos all over. One with a cute little dolphin, another a skull with snakes coming out of its eyes. There are dragons, unicorns, cars, portraits, and tons of other images all around the walls.

It's really a beautiful thing to see.

"Can I help you, pretty lady?"

I look up at the voice and glare when I see his face.

"I knew your name sounded familiar," I say. It takes all of my willpower to keep my hands on my lap when all I want to do is find something heavy and throw it as his stupid face.

"Do I know you?" he asks with that same damn grin he's always had. "I don't think I would have forgotten a pretty face like yours."

"Don't you try flattering me, you pig. I know exactly the type of man you are."

I don't answer his question because the fact that he doesn't remember who I am really hurts my heart. Not that I would ever admit that out loud, though.

"You never answered my question," he says, grin still in place. "Have we met?"

I roll my chair until I'm directly in front of him and he has to look down to keep eye contact.

"Well, it has been many years since you've seen my face," I admit, still heated. "I also wasn't in a wheelchair. Think really hard, Sammy. Think really hard about how you know me."

I've watched Sammy over the years. I know all about him and his club. I know he's called Ink, but I can never see him as anything other than Sammy.

I'm not a stalker. But I am best friends with one of the member's sister. They call him Chains, and his sister, Laura, and I have been best friends for years.

Unfortunately for me, she tells me everything about the clubs' members. I mean *everything*, including how Sammy likes to sleep with anyone with a vagina. It breaks my heart because I thought I loved him at one time.

"How do you know my real name?" he finally asks, his smirk gone. "Not many people know it, and only one person has ever called me Sammy."

I say nothing as I wait for him to figure it out.

Yep. There it is. His eyes grow wide, and he smiles.

"Rachel?" he says. "My god, you're beautiful."

I fight back the tears.

"I've changed my mind about the tattoo," I say.

I'm almost at the door when he speaks up.

"Hey, do you want to grab dinner with me?"

I stop and glare back at him.

"You expect me to have anything to do with you after the way you treated me back then?" I ask. Yes, I still hold a grudge. "You humiliated me. You took my heart, set it on fire, and stomped it beneath your feet. Do you remember any of this?"

He opens his mouth to say something, but I won't allow it.

"Let me enlighten you," I say. "Right after taking my virginity, bragging about it in front of the whole school, you turn right around and ask who you should go after next. So, no." I'm practically screaming at this point. "No, I will not go grab dinner with you."

"Rachel, sweetheart," he says, clearly upset. "I was young. I'm different now."

Just then, the curtain to some back room opens, and a tall, skinny, beautiful woman walks out.

"Thanks for the tat, Ink," she says seductively. "And thank you for the extra bonus treat."

She walks up and licks the side of his face. "I hope you were as satisfied as I was. Maybe next time you can play me a song naked."

Sammy still has his eyes glued to me, completely ignoring the newcomer.

"Yeah," I say, eyes watering. "You sure have changed. Just stay the hell away from me."

Without another word, I open the door and push myself outside. It's moments like these when I wish I could still use my legs. I would run away from this place as fast and as far as I could.

CHAPTER TWO
Ink

Holy fucking hell. Rachel Nicole Justice was just in my shop. I haven't seen that girl since high school. I have to admit that what I did back then was a pretty dick move, but come on, I was seventeen years old.

I don't care what Rachel says, I'm completely different now.

"How about you swing by my apartment when you get off work tonight. You can bring the guitar."

I shake my head to rid of the distraction that is Rachel and smile at Heather.

"No can-do babe," I say. "Got shit to do."

"Until next time," she says, seductively, before leaving.

Damn right there's going to be a next time.

I'm halfway back to my station when I notice that junior never reacted to Heather's promise.

Strange.

Usually, a promise from a willing female causes my dick to twitch with interest. Even if he was just spent.

I shove everything to the back of my mind and focus on the day's clients.

Four tattoos', and six piercings.

I love my job. I love inking up skin and I love the look of a satisfied customer. Inking women is my absolute favorite. Watching my hand gently glide over their skin while controlling the gun to ink what I want is as arousing as a woman naked in my bed.

I spend the next several hours in the zone. No thoughts enter my mind except the art and the client under my fingers at the time. It doesn't seem like long before it's time to lock up.

"Hey, do you care if I crash upstairs tonight?" Wolf asks, walking into the shop. "I need to head to my sisters in the morning and she just lives around the corner from here."

"Sure thing, brother."

Wolf helps close down the shop before we clean and sanitize the equipment. This isn't the first time he's asked to sleep here, and he always helps out when he does.

"Do anything interesting today?" Wolf asks.

"Not really," I admit. "A few basic tats and some piercings."

"What type of piercings?"

I tell him out the young woman's tongue, A Prince Albert on some guy, a couple of ears, and an Isabella piercing.

"I've heard of the Prince Albert," Wolf says. "But what the hell is an Isabella piercing?"

"To put it simply," I chuckle. "I pierced a woman's clit."

Wolf says something that I miss because I've just come to another realization. I was face and gloved knuckles deep inside of a woman's pussy an hour ago and junior still never responded.

Not even a twitch. He didn't even whimper.

"Fuck," I groan.

"What is it?" Wolf asks, completely oblivious to this life-changing moment.

"My fucking dick's broken."

◆ ◆ ◆

It's been a week. A mother fucking week, since my dick has shown interest in a single person.

"You look like you're about to explode," Chains says.

I glance down at the wrench in my hand and imagine how good it would feel to throw it at Chains' face.

"Finally run out of women?" he mocks.

Great, I decide. It would feel fucking great.

Taking a deep breath, I turn my attention back to my bike. I'm giving the girl a tune-up, then I'm taking a long ride.

Multiple phones pinging pull me from my plans.

"We're being called for Church," Chains says.

Well, hell. There goes that plan. I finish tightening the last bolt before standing.

"I'll be right there," I say, heading for the sink.

My bike is my baby. Being a Davidson Night Rod Special, she has all the personality of a Harley but with a shit-ton more power. Opening her with full throttle on a stretch of empty road is an experience I crave constantly.

Going at one-hundred and forty miles per hour feels like you're flying. I would almost say it's better than sex.

Almost.

"INK, GET THE FUCK IN HERE."

With a chuckle, I finish with my hands and follow the sound of Prez's shout.

I enter the meeting room and walk to Bear, our club

President.

I bow.

"You screamed, my lord," I say, using my fantastic British accent.

"Sit your ass down, Ink," Bear sighs.

"As you wish, master," I say. "I am your humble servant."

"Ink," Bear starts.

"Yeah, yeah," I interrupt, already knowing what he's going to say. "Shut the fuck up."

"Alright," Bear says. "Let's get started. Brick, go over the business numbers for the past week."

And there we sit, for an hour, going over bullshit numbers and projections for the following month. Same damn things we talked about at the last Church meeting. Like I've said before, we've become a domesticated biker club.

Watch out for the Infernal Sons, their domestication might rub off on you.

Yeah, we're badass, alright.

I look around at the happy faces of my brothers and want to punch them all. I used to be the only happy fucker here. What the fuck happened? Now, I've turned into Trigger.

I'm Trigger with a broken dick.

Fuck my life.

"There will be someone here tomorrow to install a pool out back," Bear grumps. "It's not a public pool, it's for family only."

"That means no fucking women in the pool, Ink," Brick smirks.

I smile, thinking that's a swell idea.

Even if my dick doesn't agree.

"Ink," Bear growls.

Before he can say anything else, Hawk's phone rings.

"It's Phoenix," he says. "He knows we're in Church, so it has to be important."

We sit silently while he answers.

"Baby, what is it?" Hawk greets.

The silence is tense as we watch Hawk's face.

"Don't provoke him, sweet boy, we'll be right there."

"What the hell is going on?" I ask, once Hawk pockets his phone.

"He's over at, Infernal Haven," Hawk says. "A man came looking for his wife and is threatening my man with bodily harm until he gives her up. He had Laura get everyone to the safe room and now he's alone with the man."

Without another word, we all jump up and head for our rides.

Infernal Haven is Slim's baby. He inherited a good bit of money from his parents and used it to open a place where people in trouble can go for help. It's helped many people and we are all incredibly proud of him.

But it doesn't come without its trouble. This type of call isn't uncommon. Most of the people at Infernal Haven are women hiding from an abusive partner.

This isn't the first time someone has come looking for their partner, and it won't be the last.

I straddle my Night Rod and make my way to the shelter. Hawk said Laura had everyone in the safe room, so that's one less thing to worry about. Laura is Chains' sister. She's a certified grief counselor who co-owns her own practice with her new fiancée`, Brad.

Whenever Slim needs the extra help, Laura doesn't hesitate to rush over and assist. She's a good woman.

It only takes five minutes to get to Infernal Haven.

Hawk pulls in seconds later followed by everyone else. Do we really need seven bikers storming in to deal with one man? No! But we make it clear that the Infernal Sons protect this building and everyone inside.

"Did Slim say if the man had any weapons?" Trigger asks.

"He told me he was just walking back and forth talking to himself," Hawk answers. "Every minute or two he would stop, demand the woman, and threaten Phoenix if he didn't bring her out."

"Don't kill the man, brother," Bear says. "Let's try to handle this calmly first and see how it goes."

With a nod, Hawk marches for the entrance.

Hawk is the most reasonable of us all. Bear's the stern one, Chains' the calm one, Trigger's the evil one, Brick's the rough one, Wolf is the new guy, and I'm the funny and most handsome one.

So, I know, without a single doubt, that Hawk will have this taken care of without a single incident.

I follow Hawk inside and freeze. A man has Slim shoved against a wall with his hands squeezing Slim's throat.

An inhuman sound reverberates around the room and I glance at Hawk in time to see him rush forward.

Well, fuck. So much for reasonable.

CHAPTER THREE
Rachel

I am so tired of these inconsiderate, rude ass people.

"Then she told me that she was going to ask his brother."

"No way! His brother?"

"Yes, way!"

I've been sitting in the middle of this isle for almost a minute now waiting on these two idiot females to kindly move to the side so I can get some dang bread. You would think after years of being confined to this chair that I would learn to speak out, but no.

It's not that I'm shy. I just don't like to feel like a burden. Which, when you depend on others for help, is an easy thing to feel.

I move my chair forward a little more hoping to catch their attention.

"There's no way I would date his brother, he isn't tall enough."

"Excuse me," I say, coming to a stop directly in front of them.

They both look down at me and then back at each other.

"Anyway," one says as if she didn't just acknowledge that I was here. "You're absolutely right. He's way too short."

"Excuse me," I say a little louder. "I really need to get behind you, please." I nod at the woman on my left hoping she will understand and just slide over a little bit.

"Rude much," she says. "Can't you see we're talking here?"

My mama always told me that I had the patience of a saint.

She was a liar. A saint has nothing on me.

"Listen," I start calmly. "I just need to grab a loaf of that bread behind you. Or you can grab it for me. Either way, it will just take a second."

"No, you listen."

"Get the fuck out of her way, bitches."

The new voice startles me, and I turn to see Sammy walking in my direction. Sammy has always been an attractive male. In high school, he had shoulder-length black hair, a pretty boy face that attracted both girls and boys, and a body that made all the football players jealous.

I was always a plain Jane. Nothing was ever special about my looks. Which is why I was surprised when he showed interest in me back then. And why I was devastated when I found out that sleeping with me was nothing more than a high school boy's idea of a game.

But now, Sammy's boyish good looks have vanished. Walking towards me now is nothing more than sex on legs. His hair is still black, but now it's faded down on the sides and long on the top. He has it styled back in a perfectly arched wave.

His eyes are dark brown, his body is lean and bulky and the white shirt that he's wearing under his club's vest is too tight around his arms. Arms that are covered in tattoos.

I find myself wondering how many tattoos he has hidden under that shirt.

"Did I stutter?" he asks, snapping me out of my daydream. "Get gone."

I turn my head back around just in time to watch the two women quickly walk away.

I'm torn. I want to thank him, and throat punch him at the same time. Instead, I move forward and grab a loaf of bread before turning around.

"Thank you for your help," I say. "Now, please, leave me alone."

I wheel my chair around him and head for a register. My stomach is rolling so much from nerves that I feel like I'm about to throw up.

What the hell is wrong with me? It's been roughly twelve years since Sammy ruined my life. I should be over it by now. But I've never been able to let it go. I've never been able to let him go.

Which is why I've never let myself get involved in another relationship. That's right, Sammy was the first and last person I've ever had sex with.

How pathetic am I?

"Rachel, wait."

Risking the bread and lunch meat from falling off my lap, I push my wheels harder to get further away from him. I can't deal with him right now.

I manage to make my way to the register and pay for my food. I'm almost outside of the store when I feel someone grab my chair from behind and give it a solid push.

I wheel around and glare at the man occupying my thoughts.

"Why did you do that?"

"There was a small rise near the door," he says, smirking. "I figured you would need help getting over it."

Oh, the nerve.

"Did I ask you for help?" I ask. "Did it look like I was struggling to get through the door?"

"Well, no," he says, smirk gone. "I just assumed it would have been difficult."

"Well, your assumptions were incorrect," I assure him. "Thank you for your help with those women, but I don't need you to help me with anything else."

"How are you getting home?" He asks.

Can he not see how uncomfortable I am around him? How can he not see the hurt in my eyes? I just want to go home and forget I ever saw him again.

"I don't live far," I explain. "I'll be fine."

"Let me take you home."

"Please, Sammy," I beg. "Please, just go. Just leave me alone."

As hard as I try to fight it, I lose the battle and a single tear tracks its way down my face.

Sammy notices it and his expression changes.

"I really fucked up with you," he says.

I look him in the eyes for a few seconds before turning and heading home. I wasn't lying. I really don't live far. I make it home in ten minutes. I put the food away and decide to take a nap.

I'm no longer craving that turkey sandwich. I just feel completely drained. Physically and emotionally.

If I never see Sam again, it will be too soon.

But, at the same time, I want him to wrap me in his arms and tell me that I'm not alone. Just like he did the night he took my heart all those years ago.

Right before he obliterated it.

Just as I'm drifting off to sleep, there's a knock on my door.

"Just a minute," I scream.

Whoever it is will have to hold their britches long enough for me to get off of this dang couch and back into my chair. I make it to the door a few minutes later and swing it open.

"Hey girlie, want to come over? Brad's heading to his grandfather's house tonight to help him move some stuff around."

My best friend Laura is standing outside of my apartment door smiling down at me. Laura is freakishly tall, so looking up at her from my chair seems like a workout at times.

"Laura," I smile. "The last time I spent the night with you we were so loud that we kept the children up and they grounded us."

Laura laughs.

"True," she admits. "But, this time, they're staying with some friends. So, it's just going to me you and me for a little girl time."

I turn and head towards my room.

"Sounds good to me," I say. "Let me pack a bag and I'll be ready to go."

This is just what I need. Something to keep my mind distracted and away from he who deserves no name.

CHAPTER FOUR
Ink

I'm a fucking stalker. I follow Rachel until she makes it home and safely inside. Since when do I give a fuck about making sure a woman gets home safely?

Maybe it's because I've known Rachel since we were in Elementary school. Yeah, that's probably it. It's an inner need to protect those that I know. That's all.

Rolling my eyes, I turn and head back to the store. Following behind her on my bike would have been obvious. So, I walked. I almost reach my ride when my phone rings.

"Yeah," I answer.

"Get back here," Bear says, sounding pissed. "We've got a fucking problem."

Hanging up, I check the time. Looks like I'm not going to open the shop today.

◆ ◆ ◆

Something big is going down. The second I made it to the clubhouse, Bear had us all rushed inside and told us to stay quiet. Now, Slim and Hawk are walking around the room with devices looking for something.

"We're all clear" Hawk says after fifteen minutes.

"What the fuck is going on?" Trigger asks the question

on all of our minds.

"Someone is threatening the club," Brick says.

"Not just the club," Bear interrupts. "Our whole fucking family."

Bear tosses a folded slip of paper onto the table. Trigger grabs it and reads it aloud.

"I'm coming for you, Sons. You better enjoy your last days in this life because I'm going to fucking kill each and every one of you. But, before I do that, I'm going to tie you down and make you watch as I kill each and every one of your fucking family members. Starting with all of those damn women and kids."

"Who the hell thought it was a good idea to threaten us?" Chains asks.

"We look like a fucking kindergarten club these days," I grump. "The only thing this club is focused on anymore is making a family. Whatever happened to throwing parties and having fun with the Bunnies?"

"We are a family, you fucking idiot," Bear growls. "We've always been a family."

"I love all of the girls and those kids," I admit. "But having them and those babies in our lives have made us weak."

"That's not true," Slim says, heated. "If anything, they've made us stronger. These men will fight tooth and nail to protect their women. Their children. How dare you call them weak."

"It's alright, sweet boy," Hawk says, rubbing his man's neck. "He just doesn't understand."

"It's not that I don't understand, brother," I say. "I would die protecting them, too. But this fucking letter just proves how vulnerable we are now. Besides, what we need to focus on now is how to keep everyone safe without causing a panic."

"I'm not sure another lockdown is the way to go," Bear says. "I'm still having nightmares from the last one."

I take a moment to remember our lost Princess. She had a bright future in front of her before it was taken away.

"Yeah," Brick whispers.

Seems like I'm not the only one remembering.

"Anything I should know?" Wolf asks.

"Not at the moment," answers Bear. "For now, we need to find out who the fuck is threatening our whole family."

"Where did you find the note?" I ask.

"I found it tucked under the edge of my bike seat an hour ago when I stopped to get gas," Bear informs us. "I already checked, and the store didn't have any working security cameras."

"The doesn't mean the surrounding buildings don't as well," Slim says, pulling out his ever-present laptop. "Which gas station was it?"

While Slim and Bear work on searching for security cameras, the rest of us compile a list of any family member that could be in danger.

It's a fucking long list.

"What about you, Ink?" Wolf asks.

"What about me?" I ask, feeling pissed.

"Your family?"

I shove the chair back and walk over to the mini bar in the corner of the room. I need a drink.

"I don't have any family," I tell him, tossing back a shot of straight vodka. "Parents died years back. I was an only child and didn't have any grandparents or aunts or uncles."

I look back and glare at the group of men looking at me

with sympathy.

"Don't look at me like that," I warn. "I've lived my life just fine without them. I have you fuckers as a family. That's all I need."

The mood in the room lifts slightly as everyone returns to what they were doing.

"Anyone else apart from your sister here, Wolf?" I ask.

"No," he answers. "Just her and her son. My family lives a good distance away."

"This is one hell of a list," Bear says, reading over our family's names. "Chains, how many kids does your sister have?"

"Three," Chains answers. "Two girls and a boy."

"So, that's eight kids total," Wolf says. "Eight little souls that someone has threatened to kill right before our eyes."

Wolf stands and punches the table. I've never seen the man lose his cool. I don't even think I've ever heard him swear before. He's so calm. But his reaction is understandable. His sister and her son are as part of this threat as everyone else.

"It won't get to that," Bear promises. "Let's sit down and make plans on how to keep our family safe. The way Ink said it was wrong, but what he said wasn't. Our family does make us vulnerable. But that's a vulnerability that I accept with open arms. We just need to show these assholes that messing with the Sons family is a big fucking mistake."

Everyone cheers and I smile.

Fucking saps.

"I found a working camera feed," Slim says, interrupting the cheer. "But you can't see who it is."

Slim does his magic and projects his computer screen

to the big screen tv we have mounted on the wall.

"You can clearly see someone walking up to Bear's bike the second he walks into the store," Slim says. "But the person is wearing a gray hoodie and there's no way to get any discerning details from this angle."

"It's definitely a male," Trigger says.

"Agreed," Chains adds. "His shoulders are too wide, and his walk is screaming male."

"That's the only camera I could get," Slim says dejectedly. "None of the other buildings had any security."

"That's alright," I tell him. "That's more information than we had a few minutes ago."

I get rewarded with a smile and I feel good knowing Slim's earlier hostility towards me has passed.

"Alright," Bear says. "We've gone over everything we can for now. Go home and call your families. Let them know what's going on and keep a lookout for anything suspicious. Supplying them with information gives them a better chance than if they knew nothing at all."

Once we're dismissed, I hop up and head towards the door. I'm determined to get my dick wet tonight. I need a distraction from everything so that I can come back tomorrow completely focused.

"Mother fucker," Chains yells. "I have five missed calls from my sister."

"Call her back now," Bear says. "From now on, no more muted cells during church until we figure this shit out."

"Laura," Chains says frantically. "What's wrong?"

We wait in tense silence while she answers.

"Slow down, I can't understand you."

Chains pulls the phone from his ear and pushes the speaker button.

"And when I opened it... Blake, there was blood everywhere. It was on… and it covered."

"We'll be there in fifteen minutes, sweetheart," Bear says. "Just try and stay calm. Where are the babies?"

"Th…they're staying with some friends for the night," Laura says. "Brad went to help his grandfather, so he isn't here either."

"Alright sis," Chains says softly. "We'll be there soon."

"Please hurry," Laura whispers before hanging up.

Sorry junior. Looks like you're not getting wet after all. Not that you would have cooperated anyway, you little fuck.

CHAPTER FIVE
Rachel

"I see that Brad doesn't skimp on the good stuff," I say, sipping my wine.

Laura laughs and pours her second glass.

"Girl, he knows better," she says. "My wine is the only luxury I allow myself. Between my three kids and my clients, cheap wine won't do shit for me."

"I could only imagine," I admit. "I spend my time behind a computer screen designing websites. I don't have to deal with a single person face-to-face."

"Lucky bitch."

"Tell me about it," I laugh. "You're the only person I actually like. Well, you, Brad, and the kids. The rest of the world are jerks."

"Including Ink?"

"Ink who?" I ask, trying to sound ignorant.

"Don't try and act stupid," she says, catching my game. "I see how you pay extra close attention whenever I bring him up in conversation. Why do you think I do it more than the other bikers for?"

I stare at her shocked.

"You are one evil woman," I say.

She tosses her head back, laughing.

A knock on the door interrupts our fun.

"Who is it?" Laura yells.

"You have a peephole," I say. "And you can actually reach it."

Laura's eyes widen and she says, "Have you ever seen those horror movies where someone looks through the peephole only to be shot or have a giant needle shoved into their eye?"

"Uhm, no?"

"FedEx," someone says from outside. "I have a package."

Laura opens the door and accepts a medium-sized box.

"Thank you," she tells the delivery person before shutting the door.

"Can you hold this while I go get a knife?" she asks.

I nod and place the box on my lap. Whatever is inside is pretty heavy.

"Were you expecting something?" I yell.

"Nope," Laura says, coming back into the living room.

"I can't find a return address anywhere," I say.

"Well, let's open it up and see what it is."

With the box still sitting in my lap, Laura shoves the knife through the center of the tape and cuts the seal. We open the flaps and find a black container inside surrounded by saran wrap.

"Well, this just became some Dexter shit," Laura says.

"Maybe we shouldn't open that," I say.

My gut is telling me that something isn't right.

"You're probably right," Laura says, smirking.

"You're going to do it, anyway, aren't you?"

"You betcha sweet patootie."

I smile and roll my eyes. Laura is always a risk-taker.

"Can you at least get it off of my la…"

Before I can finish my sentence, Laura has already grabbed the container out of the box, shoved the box to the floor, and flopped the suspiciously heavy, black container back onto my lap.

"I am not a table, woman," I chide like always when she uses me for a table.

It really never bothers me. We joke about it often. She uses me for a table, I use her for arms to reach things I can't. It works for us.

But, right now, I really don't want to be her table.

"Just let me get this open and I'll move it."

She cuts away the plastic wrap and opens the lid. I'm blasted with a horrid smell that turns my stomach and causes my gag reflex to react instantly.

"Oh, my god, what the hell is that?" I scream.

Laura finishes removing the lid and we both scream. The container isn't black. It's a clear container filled to the brim with blood. I jerk back, trying to get away when the container tips over and spills all over my legs.

"What the fuck is that?" Laura screeches.

I look up to see that she's pointing at my lap.

"Blood, Laura," I yell. "It's freaking blood."

"No, Rachel. That."

I follow her finger and that's when I see it.

"Oh god, it's a freaking tongue," I cry.

I'm starting to panic. I want to get out of these clothes, to get out of this chair and into a shower. But I can't move.

"Laura, I need you to help me to the shower," I beg.

She nods her head and finally shoves the container off of my lap. My hands have been frozen against my wheels this whole time.

"Wait, is that a note?" Laura asks.

She walks over to where she tossed the box and picks up a sheet of paper.

"What's it say?" I ask, trying to stay calm but knowing that I'm seconds away from having a complete meltdown.

"It says, *I Think you will be my first. Tell the Sons I say, hi,*" she reads. "It's signed, HC."

"Just, HC?" I ask.

"I need to call my brother."

I nod my head knowing she's right. As much as I want to take a shower and scold my skin with boiling water, maybe calling her brother first would be a good move.

Ink

It takes us less than fifteen minutes to arrive at Laura's house. I've met Laura many times, but my gut is telling me that this time will change my life as I know it.

"LAURA," Chains screams the moment our bikes are off.

"In here," she yells back. "I don't want to leave her. We're in the living room."

I follow Chains into the house, and we make our way to the living room. The first thing I see is Laura's hands covered in blood and holding a sheet of paper out of Chains.

I step around Chains and stop in my tracks. Rachel is sitting in her chair in the middle of the floor covered in blood. All rational thought escapes my body and I rush forward.

"What the fuck happened?" I ask, slamming to my knees. My eyes are searching her body for an injury only to find none.

"Where's the blood coming from, baby," I ask, ignoring that little term of endearment. "Where are you hurt?"

I want to run my hands over her body to find the injury

but I'm afraid that it could only make it worse.

"It's not my blood," Rachel says, her voice small and scared. So different from the fierce sound that she spoke to me with earlier.

"Ink, read this," Chains says.

I reach my hand out, not ready to move away from Rachel.

Once Chains hands me the note, I read it and see red.

"We may not have a choice," I tell the room. All of my brothers finally arrived and are in the living room watching the scene unfold. "Prez, we're going to have to go into lockdown. Shit just got real."

Bear's face is grim as he nods with determination.

"Let's get everything prepared," Bear says. "Time to protect our family."

I glance back down to Rachel whose face has gone blank.

"If someone could please get this dang tongue off of my lap, I would really like to shower and go home."

I look down and sure enough, a human tongue is sitting right on her leg. We get the tongue back in the container and Laura helps Rachel into the bathroom.

Rachel is about to be naked only feet away from me. What a wonderful sight that would be.

My jeans become tight for the first time in over a week.

Fuck no, junior. We don't get hard for only a single person.

But I'd be lying if I said the thought of waking up to Rachel every single morning isn't something that I've been thinking about since she walked into my shop.

Damn it all to hell.

CHAPTER SIX
Rachel

"Rachel, please reconsider," Laura says for the fifth time.

The club is going into lockdown and that means that they bring in their family. I guess it only happens when something dangerous could happen and that's understandable.

What I don't understand is why this woman won't leave me alone about it.

"Laura, I have no affiliation with that club," I repeat. "I'm perfectly safe here in the outside world. Not a single soul is going to connect me to any of you."

It takes another half an hour to finally convince Laura that I will be fine. She can be a pain in the butt from time to time. But I love her for it.

I pull my chair up to my work desk and power up my computer. Might as well get some work done. I'm not sure how much time passes when there's a knock at my door.

"Coming," I yell.

When I get to the door I reach up for the handle and swing it open.

"You didn't check to see who it was."

"I thought you were in lockdown?" I ask the grumpy looking Sammy. "And how do you know where I live?"

"I followed you home the other night," he admits. "You didn't answer my question."

"It wasn't a question," I say, rolling my eyes, not a bit surprised by his answer. "But, to acknowledge your statement, the peephole is way up there, and I am way down here. And I'm not sure if you noticed or not, but my legs don't work anymore."

"You could have simply asked who it was," he says, inviting himself into my apartment.

"And ruin the surprise?" I say sarcastically. "What fun would that be?"

I watch as Sammy makes his way around my apartment as if he owns the place.

"Is there something I can help you with, Sam?" I ask, aggravated, as he noses through my cabinets.

"Why aren't you at the club?" he asks.

Sammy turns and leans on the kitchen counter, arms and legs crossed.

"What reason would I have to be there?" I ask confused.

"Like you said, we're in lockdown."

"What is it with you and Laura all of a sudden?" I ask. "Neither of you have ever involved me in club issues before. Why now?"

"There's shit going down and you could be in danger just like the rest of us."

Sighing, I go to the fridge and grab a water. I'm getting a headache and I need my freaking drugs if I have to deal with this man a minute longer.

"Listen, Ink, just go back to your family and your women and let me live my life in peace," I beg. "I have nothing to do with your club so there is no danger to me. The only connection I even have to it is Laura and she is only connected because of her brother."

"Let's get a few things straight," a very pissed off man says. "First off, everyone else calls me Ink. You call me, Sammy. Got it?"

Electricity shoots through my core at how sexy he sounds. Damn traitorous body.

I nod.

"Second, you are connected to the club through Laura and through me. So, yes, there is a danger to you. Now, go pack your shit and let's go."

My hands automatically go to my wheels to do as Sammy demanded but my rational brain finally kicks in and I stop.

"I'm not going anywhere with you, Sam," I say. "I wouldn't trust you to hold my bag let alone put my life in your hands. If there's ever a time when I feel as if my life is in danger, I'll just go to the police."

"The police are useless," he says, heated.

"Maybe," I say. "But at least I know for a fact they won't just use me then toss me aside to sample the person next in line."

Okay, so that made no sense whatsoever, but I don't care. He understands what I'm talking about.

"Fine," he huffs. "But know that I'll be by here each and every day to check on you."

I go to my kitchen table and grab my bottle of pain relievers. I feel a migraine coming on and it's going to be a big one.

"I thought the whole point of a lockdown was to be locked down," I say. "I doubt your President would allow you in and out of your compound whenever you want when there's danger afoot."

Sammy smiles.

"Afoot?" he teases. "Prez would kick me out just to get me to shut up. Don't you worry, pretty lady. I'll be back."

That's what I'm afraid of.

"Whatever," I mumble. "Listen, I have a major headache coming on. Would you please leave so I can sleep it off before it gets too bad? Oh, and do me a favor?"

"Name it, pretty lady," he smirks.

"One," I start. "Stop calling me pretty lady. Laura says that's how you flirt and that's the last thing I want. Two," I turn and head towards my room. "Lock the door on your way out. And last, please don't ever come back."

I don't wait around for his response, but I do wait by my bedroom door until I hear his heavy footfalls leave. I don't dare move until I hear the click of the door. Then I wait a few more minutes before I venture out of my room to go and lock the deadbolt.

I hate that I'm pushing Sammy away. But there's no way that I could trust him enough to even be friends with him. Sure, he was young and dumb. But, in all honesty, he hasn't changed all that much.

I just hope he wasn't telling the truth about showing up every day to check on me.

◆ ◆ ◆

He was telling the truth.

It's been three days since he warned me and true to his word, he's been here each day with lunch. And each day I've tried to pay him for my lunch and kicked him out.

Today makes day four.

"Come out to lunch with me," he says. "I'll take you wherever you want to go."

Sighing, I go back to folding my laundry.

I don't go out much. I'll go to the store when I need to, or to Laura's when she forces me. But apart from that, I don't leave. I prefer it that way. My home is my safe place.

I don't 'people' very well. People stare and they pity. I hate pity. Don't freaking pity me.

Strangely, Sammy doesn't look at me with pity. He looks at me with, dare I say, interest. I think it's because I'm the only female on the face of the planet that doesn't jump on his face when he smirks.

Not that I don't want to, mind you.

Been there, done that. Know how amazing he was as a freaking teenager. But I just can't seem to get past the part where I was just a notch on his bedpost.

"Listen, just lunch," he says. "Then, I'll bring you right back here."

I want to say no but getting out of this apartment sounds like a really good idea.

"Fine," I relent. "But I get to choose."

"Deal," he smiles.

"You didn't bring your bike, did you?" I ask. "Because I won't be able to use my legs to hold on."

"Don't worry, baby," he says, taking my keys and locking the apartment door. "I have everything under control."

CHAPTER SEVEN
Ink

R achel is one stubborn ass woman.

"Why won't you let me help you in the car?" I ask.

"If I let everyone do everything for me," she says. "Then how am I ever going to be able to do anything for myself? Besides, I've been in this chair for years now. I know what the hell I'm doing."

I chuckle, raise my hands in surrender, and back away. I watch in awe at the amount of upper body strength it takes to move herself from her chair to the front seat of the car in no time flat.

"Now you can help if you want," she says with a smile. I suddenly feel like my life's mission is to put that smile on her face every moment of every day.

What the fuck is happening to me?

"Trunk?" I ask.

"Yep. Do you know how to fold it?"

I nod my head and push her chair to the back of the car. Truthfully, I have no fucking idea what I'm doing. But how hard can it be? Five minutes go by and I can hear Rachel laughing.

She explains how to fold the damn chair through her giggles which brings a smile to my face.

Damn it all to hell. I feel the domestication taking root.

Rachel

The car ride over to the restaurant was done in silence. Not the type of silence that makes you shift in your seat but the type that lets you completely relax in comfort instead.

Which is weird, considering every time I thought about Sammy in the past, I was shoved back to that high school day.

"Where do you want to sit?" Sammy asks as we make our way into a popular Mom and Pop restaurant.

"It doesn't matter," I say. "As long as the table is low enough for me to actually reach my food."

Sammy laughs and guides me to a booth near the back of the dining room.

We get settled in and a waitress comes to take our orders.

I'm stuck in this fantasy with Sammy that I don't want to escape from. Maybe he really is different. Maybe Laura overexaggerated when she would tell me stories about his sexcapades.

I mean, no one could really sleep with that many people, right? Not that I'm judging him. I guess it always bothered me because I've never gotten over the man. I fell in love with Sammy when I was a teenager and I never stopped loving him.

Or rather, I never stopped loving the person I knew he could be.

"Ink, is that you?"

I'm brought out of my daydream by a high-pitched squeal as a long-legged blondie jumps right into Sammy's lap.

"My goodness, it's been ages," she giggles.

"Get the fuck off of me, woman," Sammy grunts. "Can't you see I'm on a date?"

Did he just date?

"You don't date," the woman laughs. "Everyone knows that. You must be his newest conquest," she says, looking down at my chair. "Although, I don't see why. You won't be able to do much but lay there. What fun would that be?"

"Woman, you better fucking apologize right fucking now."

I hear Sammy and the woman bicker back and forth, but I pay them no attention. Mainly because the woman's right. I've always blamed what Sammy did to me on the reason why I've never slept with another man but that isn't the whole truth.

What the woman said is another huge part of it. I can't do anything but lay there. What man would want to be with a woman who can only lay in bed like a freaking potato while he does all the work?

I'm still zoned out when the woman says something and storms off.

Sammy grips my chin and forces me to look at him which brings my focus back to reality.

"Did you hear what I said?" he asks.

I shake my head, too afraid to talk.

"I said, don't listen to a fucking word that bitch says. You're absolutely perfect the way you are. Any man would be lucky to have you as his woman."

"Except you, right?" I think.

Except, Sammy's eyes grow wide and I realize that I didn't just think those words.

"I d...di.."

I'm saved from my stuttering mess when the waitress places our food on the table.

"Is there anything else I can get for you?" she asks. Her eyes and flirtatious smile glued to Sammy's face.

"No thank you," I answer, much to her disappointment.

I start shoving my cheeseburger into my mouth to keep it from spouting off any more stupid crap.

What the hell is wrong with me? I despise this man. Right?

Right?

"You're wrong, you know?" Sammy says.

"About what?" I ask with a mouth full of food.

He smiles.

"About me not bei..."

"Hey, Ink."

"For fuck's sake," Sammy sighs.

I look over and, sure enough, another woman is standing by his side.

"Are you busy later?" she asks.

"Yes, I am," he growls. "Now fuck off. Come on, baby. We're leaving."

"But my friends are here," the woman whines. "The same ones from last time."

I try to hold back my smile as I continue eating my lunch. It doesn't look like Sammy likes his past conquests barging into his life while he's trying to enjoy his lunch.

Sure, I'm jealous. I'm not afraid to admit it. But Sammy is who he is. He's not going to change for anyone. I've accepted that a long time ago. It doesn't mean my feelings for him have changed. It just means that I can despise him loudly and love him quietly.

I finish my burger and fries while Sammy and the new chick argue about something.

"Fucking fine," Sammy shouts. "I'll be over there in a minute."

With a satisfied smile, the woman walks to the other side of the room where her waiting friends must be.

"I need to go take care of this shit really quick, baby," he tells me, much calmer than he was a few seconds ago. "It will only take a few minutes."

I don't say anything, but I do nod.

"Don't move," he says. "I'll be right back."

He stands, kisses my forehead, and walks away. I'm momentarily shocked at the sweet move but I'm not the only one. Sammy pauses for a second, throws a confused look back at me before walking away.

I bask at the butterflies swarming my belly for only a moment before crushing their tiny souls. I will not get myself wrapped up in this man again.

I sit here for ten minutes and he still hasn't returned. Whatever those women wanted to talk to him about must have been really interesting to keep his attention.

I wait another five minutes before I toss money on the table, ping a taxi, and head outside to wait for my ride.

When the taxi pulls in some time later, I glance back through the restaurant window to see our table still empty.

Just as well. I needed the reminder of who this man is. Of what he's capable of. The small piece of wall around my heart that he knocked down with this lunch and that sweet kiss was just fortified by his actions.

I'll continue to despise him loudly.

But I'll always love him soundlessly.

Why is that suddenly not enough?

CHAPTER EIGHT
Ink

F ucking bitch. How fucking stupid does she think I am?

"It's true, Ink," she whines. "I'm pregnant."

I have to keep reminding myself that I don't hit women.

"I wouldn't doubt if you were pregnant, but I know for a mother fucking fact that it's not mine," I say for the tenth time.

"You're the only person I've slept with in months," she says. "It has to be yours. I remember that night like it was yesterday. We didn't use protection."

I don't fucking hit women.

"I haven't seen you in ten months, Lily," I remind her. "And, in case I'm mistaken, if you were pregnant with my child, that baby would have already been born. Also, I always use a condom. I buy my own, I apply my own, and I discard my own. I'm not fucking stupid. But nice try."

Lily starts more of her annoying whining, but I ignore her and walk back to my woman.

Fuck.

I mean, my table.

When I arrive at an empty table, I fucking panic. Damnit. What's wrong with me? There's someone going after the club and our families. Why would I leave her alone?

"Can I get you anything else?"

I look up to see the waitress smiling.

"Where did the woman go that was with me?" I ask.

"Oh," she says, her smile falling. "She left with another man."

"What?"

"Bro, she got in a taxi," a man says from the next table. "Why the hell do women do that?" He glares at the waitress. "It only makes you sound desperate. And no one wants a desperate woman."

I nod my head at the man and toss a fifty on the table to pay for our food. I'm heading for the door when a last-minute thought pops in my head.

"How long was she sitting here waiting for me?" I ask the man.

"Twenty minutes, maybe," he answers.

Twenty fucking minutes?

Damnit.

"Thank you," I say.

I'm going to have to break her door down. That's the only way I'm getting into her apartment because there is no way in hell she will open her door for me.

◆ ◆ ◆

"Rachel, please open the door," I beg for the hundredth time in thirty minutes. "I can explain, baby. Please, just open the door."

Nothing. She hasn't said a single word. She is so pissed that I can taste it from out here.

"I'm just going to sit out here until you open this door,"

I warn. "One way or another, you will come out and talk to me."

I sit on the damn concrete porch for another half an hour before I finally lose my temper.

Standing, I pound on the door. "Rachel, open this fucking door or I'm going to break it down."

"You will do no such thing," Rachel says from behind me.

"You do have a logical reason for beating my door, right?" she asks. "Because I don't know if you can tell, but I live in an apartment complex. There are occupied apartments on either side of mine, and they have their nosy little faces pressed up against the windows."

"Where have you been?" I ask, ignoring everything else. Now that I know she's been out and about alone this whole time I'm freaking out for a whole different reason.

What the fuck is wrong with me? My dick isn't the only thing broken. My brain is, too.

"To get groceries," she says, looking confused.

Not that I blame her. I'm confusing myself, sweetheart.

"Why did you leave?" I ask, much calmer than before.

She sighs. "I was finished eating and you were preoccupied."

"I can explain," I say.

"Sam," she interrupts. "You don't have to explain anything to me. I have no holds over your life."

God, if that were only true.

"She tried to con me," I explain anyway. "She said I was the father of her unborn child."

Rachel's eyes widen and mist over slightly before she looks away. I saw hurt there. I know I did.

"And are you?" she asks.

"Of course not," I answer. "I have no children. I have

always been extremely cautious when it comes to protection. Plus, the last time I had sex with her was almost a year ago. She's fucking insane."

That hurtful look passes her eyes again before she pushes her chair forward and unlocks her door.

"That's good then," she says roughly. "Thank you for lunch, Sammy. It was surprisingly nice to spend some time with you."

I smile.

"Well, with you and a few of the women that you've had sex with."

I frown and Rachel laughs.

"Consider my ass bitten," I mumble.

"What was that?"

"Nothing," I say louder.

The guys are always telling me that sleeping with so many women will come back to bite me in the ass one day. Well, day, meet ass.

I have to accept the truth. I want Rachel. And not just for a night or a monthly tumble in the sheets. For life. I want to marry this woman. I want her to have my babies. I want to grow old and die with her.

But I can practically feel the brick wall she's built between us. And it's because adult Ink is no more mature than teenage Sammy was.

What the hell do I have to do to gain this woman's heart?

"Go out with me," I say on a whim, shutting her door behind us.

"We just went out, Sammy," she laughs. "I know I have a little booty fluff but I'm not hungry just yet."

"No," I smile. "Go out with me. You know, wear my cut. Be my ol' lady."

Holy hell, this is hard. How do men do it?

The color drains from her face. A reaction I was fully expecting.

"What game are you playing, Sam?" she asks, her eyes misting.

"No game, baby," I say, kneeling down and placing my hands on her knees.

We're just inside the apartment with the door shut. Rachel still has her purse around her shoulder and grocery bags on her lap.

"I really mean it," I admit. "I've been fighting this feeling since you came into my shop. I can't do it anymore. I don't want to."

"Sam, there are so many obstacles between us that a relationship would never be possible," she says quietly.

"I don't believe that for a second," I tell her. "And I'm going to prove it to you. Give me one obstacle."

"High school," she says quickly.

"I meant it when I said, I've changed. Maybe it wasn't completely true at my shop," I admit. "But I swear to you that it is now. No other woman has interested me since you came back into my life. And at the risk of sounding like a complete dick, I've tried, baby. I've tried to find interest in other women. But I can't. Because none of them are you."

I reach out with my thumb and gently wipe away her falling tears.

"Give me another," I demand.

Her tears fall faster.

"My legs," she says so softly that I almost miss it.

I move the bags from her lap to the floor.

"These legs?" I ask, rubbing the exposed skin not covered by her shorts. "These legs are very sexy," I admit.

"They're so soft, so pale and creamy so…"

"Dead," she interrupts forcefully. "They're useless, dead limbs, Sam. That's all they will ever be. How come you've never asked me why I was in this chair? Surely you remember that I used to be able to walk."

"I remember, baby."

"Stop calling me that," she yells.

She grips her wheels and pulls away from me.

"What you think you want isn't going to happen," she says. "Just go home, Sammy. Forget about me again. Life was better that way."

Rachel turns and heads for her living room. Her apartment is open to most rooms, so I watch as she moves her chair to the couch and slides over to sit in the corner. All I can see is her beautiful brown hair flowing over the arm of the sofa.

"What do you mean by 'what I think I want?'" I ask as she turns on the tv.

She doesn't say anything at first but continues to search for something to watch. After an eternity, she finally flips off the tv and sighs.

"It's no surprise that women fall at your feet, Sammy," she says, softly. "All it takes is half a smile and you have women, and some men, under your control. And, of course, they say yes."

Rachel moves around until she's looking me in the eyes.

"Then you have me. Someone whose heart was taken years ago by a boy. A boy who broke it and never gave it back. And I tell you no. Something you don't hear. A challenge. That's what you want, Sam, the challenge. Not the person. Not me."

Part of me wants to scream and yell that she's wrong.

And another part wants to jump for joy at what she's admitted.

"Do you want your heart back, baby?" I whisper as I walk closer. "You're wrong, you know. You told me to forget about you...again. That life was better that way." I stop just a foot from the couch. "I've been thinking about this a lot these past few days. About why I've slept with so many women over the years."

"God, Sam, I don't want to hear this," Rachel says, turning around.

I move to sit on the coffee table in front of where she's sitting.

"Let me finish," I demand. "I used to think it was because I never wanted to settle down. I wanted to be a free man for the rest of my life. But, as I went back to the clubhouse the past few nights, without you, I've realized it's because there was a void missing that I was trying to fill.

I had felt something once that I was trying to get back. But I could never find it. Then you came into my shop looking for a tattoo and everything clicked into place. I fought the fuck out of it, babe. No way in hell was I going to be that guy.

But there's no questioning it. You are the missing void. So, like I said, you're wrong. I never forgot about you. You have always been part of me. I was just too fucked up to see the truth. So, I'll ask you again, do you want your heart back?"

I sit back and watch as the emotions play across her face. I hope that what I said was the key to opening this woman's heart to me. Because I will let her domesticate the hell out of me if she agrees to be mine.

White picket fence, here we come.

I hope.

CHAPTER NINE
Rachel

How do I even respond to that? I'm sure my mouth and eyes are both wide as my brain strains to find something to say.

You hate Sam. You hate Sam. You hate Sam.

No matter how many times I remind myself, it doesn't stick. His words are what I've longed to hear from him for years. So, why the heck am I not telling him that?

He doesn't say anything as I process the crazy amount of information firing through my brain.

Is he making fun of me? He never really answered my question about my legs, did he? Did he avoid it on purpose?

"I'll never walk again," I finally say, my voice strangely clear and strong despite my inner hurricane. "I'll never have a normal relationship with someone because I require special things for my day-to-day life. Equipment that tends to get in the way. I'll never be able to ride on your bike because I won't be able to properly hold on. I won't be able to stand up and dance at my wedding or run after my kids if they're in danger.

Life with me is not easy. It's a challenge. I'm a challenge, Sammy. And until I know for a fact that what you really want is me and not the challenge, then I can't bring myself to believe your words."

I don't look away. I want this man to know deep down in my soul how hard these words are.

"I want to hate you," I admit. "I want to hold on to that grudge from all those years ago. But I fell in love with you when we were teenagers and that feeling never went away. Not really."

Sammy leans forward and brushes more of the tears off my face.

"I think we both need time to really think about things," I regretfully admit. "Please, go, Sammy. And don't come back until you are one-hundred percent sure of what you want."

He starts to say something, but I quickly lean forward and press my lips against the corner of his mouth.

I pull back before he has time to react.

"Twenty-four hours," I say. "Think about what you want for twenty-four hours. Think about it hard. Until then, hold on to my broken heart. You can either bring it back to me fixed with the realization that you mean every word you said.

Or you can bring it back to me healed, knowing that I can finally leave the past where it is and move on to a new and different future. Without you."

Sammy looks at me with such intensity that I fear he's already made up his mind. But he simply stands, kisses my forehead, and leaves my apartment, shutting the door behind him.

I'm not sure how long I sit on the couch just watching the door. Do I want him to come back in or am I afraid that it's the last time I'll ever see him?

My own feelings confuse me.

I maneuver my way onto my chair and go to lock the door.

It's then that I hear heavy footsteps walk away.
I roll my eyes and smile.
Caveman.

Ink

Arguing with Rachel would be useless. I've already made up my mind. I know what I want. She's all I've thought about since the day she entered my shop.

"No Rachel again, today?" Laura asks when I settle down in the family room of the clubhouse.

"Stubborn woman," I smile.

"I'm still trying to wrap my mind around you going after a single woman," Brick smirks. "She must be something."

"She is," I agree. "And I think I've finally got her where I want her. She seems to think what I'm feeling is about the challenge. But what I'm feeling is an obsession I have never before felt. The only challenge I'm facing is getting her to understand that I mean every word I say to her."

I look around at my brothers and their partners. I remember doing this same thing not long ago and rolling my eyes at how domesticated we've become. Now, all I can think about is Rachel by my side as we talk to our family.

"I'm happy for you, brother," Chains says. "I've met Rachel a few times over at my sisters and I can honestly say that she's an amazing person."

I smile and clap Chains' shoulder.

"Alright, let's talk about Ink's woman later," Bear says with a grin. "Slim has some news. I won't be calling church," he amplifies his voice so everyone can hear. "Because like I always say, it's best to have everyone informed of the danger so they know to look out for it."

I watch as Rose and Bella gather all seven kids, including Laura's, and take them out of the room.

"I contacted some friends of mine that were able to discretely run a DNA scan on the blood and tongue that was left at Laura's place," Slim starts. "I'm still waiting on a response to see if there was a hit with an ID, but I did learn what we all assumed. The blood is human."

"How can that be?" Laura asks. "It was the same color and consistency as human blood, but it shouldn't have been. Blood coagulates after a while. If that was human blood it shouldn't have been so thin."

"Unless it was less than a day old," I say, gritting my teeth with the reminder of Rachel's legs covered in the blood.

"Exactly," Slim adds. "While we don't know whose blood and tongue it was, we do know that the person died less than a day before the package was delivered to Laura."

"This person was most likely a random kill meant to spook us," Brick says, pulling Jessa tighter against his chest. "My guess is that it was someone homeless that no one will even notice is missing."

I nod in agreement.

"Well, we do have one other clue," Hawk says. "The note at Laura's was signed, HC. It's not much but it's a start."

"A start that I was able to work off of," Slim says. "I've been searching any enemies we might have with those initials but haven't come up with anything. Once my friends get me the info on the owner of the blood and tongue, I'll start searching there as well."

The Sons don't really have any enemies but I'm sure there are a few people out there who don't like us much.

Hopefully, we can figure this shit out soon. The thought of my woman, yes, *my woman,* out there alone right now has me stressing more than ever.

"What about each of us as individuals?" Slim asks. "It would take a few days, but I could dig into all of our backgrounds and see if I can match those initials with someone from one of our pasts."

"Whoever is doing this is after the club as a whole," Bear says. "It wouldn't hurt for you to look into it, but I don't think you'll find anything."

Slim nods and walks back to Bear's office where he's set up his equipment.

"If you need to leave this building for anything," Bear says to the room. "Don't do it alone."

With our Prez's final word, everyone goes back to doing their own thing.

I pull out my phone and text Rachel, silently laughing at her reaction when she finds out what I've done to my contact name in her phone.

Hey baby, just so you know, my decision about wanting you in my life has only gotten stronger this past hour. But I'll give you the day you've asked for. Expect me there this time tomorrow. Have sweet dreams, beautiful.

"Ink, can you hold Daisy for a minute?" Rose asks as I'm tucking my phone back into my pocket.

"Well, of course, I will hold this pretty little lady," I say, snatching little Daisy from Rose's arms. "Come with uncle Ink and I'll tell you some deep secret shit about your daddy."

Rose laughs as I walk away.

Yeah, I was an idiot before. I can't wait for the domesticated life to take hold of me.

CHAPTER TEN
Rachel

S**exy Stud Muffin**: *Hey baby, just so you know, my decision about wanting you in my life has only gotten stronger this past hour. But I'll give you the day you've asked for. Expect me there this time tomorrow. Have sweet dreams, beautiful.*

I don't know if I want to laugh or scream at the incoming text. For one, I know exactly who Sexy Stud Muffin is. Also, I never gave him my number and I don't remember a time when he was able to take my phone without my noticing.

Two can play this game.

I'm sorry, but this time tomorrow isn't going to work. I forgot that I promised a friend that I would go on a double date with her, her boyfriend and his brother. Can we shoot for the day after?

With a satisfied smile, I decide to find something to read as I wait for him to respond. Time for a good book to escape into. As I reach for my kindle on the bedside table, I knock off my charger cord and bottle of water. Not the first time I've done that and I'm sure it won't be the last.

I'm about to make my way to the floor to pick them up when my phone rings. Already knowing who it is, I answer without looking and lay back down.

"Hey, there, Stud Muffin," I answer, trying my best to

hold back a giggle.

"You are damn lucky that I have a baby in my arms, or I'd be on my way over there to tie you down."

The anger in his voice wipes the smile off my face. What the heck?

"You afraid I'm going to run away?" I tease, trying to lighten the moon.

"That's exactly what I'm afraid of," he says. "Until you decide if you want to give us a chance, no double dates with anyone."

I freeze, realizing why he sounds so angry.

"I was only teasing," I say gently. "I don't really have a double date. Even if I did, I would likely bail."

Sammy's quiet and I hear the soft sounds of the baby in his arms. I wonder whose baby it is. I wonder if he's had sex with the baby's mother.

"Aren't you supposed to be in lockdown?" I ask, trying my best to push the jealousy aside.

"I am," he finally says. "I'm surrounded by people at this very moment. None of them are you and it's making me pissy."

I smile. "You probably shouldn't curse in front of the baby," I say.

"Don't worry about pretty Daisy," he says. I can hear the fondness in his voice. "Between me, her daddy, and these other fucks, her first word will indeed be, 'fuck'."

"I wouldn't doubt it for a second," I hear a woman say. "Thank you, Ink. You're the best."

"No problem, pretty Rose. Anytime you want me to hold that girl just shove her in my arms."

The woman laughs and I have the urge to go over there and punch her in the face. This is one of the reasons why I told him to stop calling me, pretty lady. He calls every single female pretty and I hated that I didn't feel special when he said it to me.

Hearing "pretty Rose" laugh just proves my point.

I know who Rose is. When she first arrived, Laura was concerned for the club's president, Bear. Apparently, he took a quick liking to the woman. Everything worked itself out in the end, though.

Even though I know who she is and that she's a married woman, it doesn't stop the insane amount of envy and jealousy that sweeps through my body.

"Baby, did you hear me?"

"I'm sorry," I say, mentally smacking myself. "What did you say?"

"I said your teasing needs a little work," he chuckles. "It might get a man hurt one of these days."

"Oh, you wouldn't have done a single thing if I did have a date," I say.

The humor completely leaves Sammy's voice when he growls, "Let's not find out."

Okay, so maybe he would have.

"Get some sleep, babe. I've got club shit to do. Like I said, expect me there tomorrow night. You have between now and then to get any sort of doubt out of your head. Because this thing between you and me, it's happening."

"There's a thing?" I ask breathlessly. Because he sounds so sure of our future being entwined.

"Go to sleep, beautiful."

"Okay," I whisper. What else am I supposed to say?

I'm about the push the 'end call' button when I put the phone back up to my ear.

"Sammy, do you call all the other women beautiful?"

He's quiet and I can feel the blush take over my face.

Why the heck did I ask that? That jealous feeling of not having a special name just for me makes me sick. Why would he have a special name for me? I'm no one important.

"The only other woman I've called beautiful was my mama," he says, softly. "I don't call anyone baby or beautiful. Those are yours, sweetheart. Never again will a single soul come before you. I really hope you trust yourself to believe me. Now, get to sleep and I'll see you tomorrow."

"Okay, night," I blindly say.

I end the call and close my eyes. I have a lot to think about and not very much time to do it. I also know thinking about anything is just a waste of time. I already know I'm going to give Sammy a go.

I've loved that man for as long as I can remember. What's that saying? If you love something let it go and if it comes back it was meant to be?

I may not have let Sammy go all those years ago, but we did end up going our separate ways. Me with a broken heart. Him, with confused feelings.

Well, here we are, years later, the same two people. Only, different.

I don't know how long I lay in my bed just thinking about the past and possible future, but I eventually fall asleep with a smile on my face and hope in my heart.

***

BANG!

I'm jerked out of sleep by a loud noise. I sit up in bed and listen but can't hear anything else. Maybe the sound was actually in my dream. It wouldn't be the first time a dream woke me up and I'm sure it won't be the last.

I lay back down and close my eyes.

I can't even remember what I was dreaming about. That usually happens when I'm awoken suddenly.

I'm about to drift off when I hear it again.

BANG!

"Okay, not a dream," I whisper.

The walls between apartments aren't all that thick and I can hear all sorts of interesting things from time to time. But this didn't sound like it came from another apartment. It sounded like it came from the other room.

I go to grab my phone only to notice it still on my bed. I quickly pick it up and push the button to wake it. I need to call the police.

The screen remains back. It's dead and my charger is still on the floor completely out of reach.

"Damnit,"

I move my legs to the side of the bed and start shuffling my way to the edge as quietly as I can. I need that damn charger. I need to find a way to make it to the floor without making a sound. I knock my charger cord off all the time so I'm no stranger to falling to the floor to get it, but my body flops down from the bed and I know that's going to make noise.

"Hands first," I whisper to myself.

I pull my legs back onto the bed and start pulling myself off the bed arms and head, first. This way I have more control over my body. I finally manage to make my way to the floor with the feet still resting up on the bed.

I grab my pajama pants and lift one leg down before doing the same to the other.

Holy crap, I'm exhausted.

I turn and grab the charger cord and internally curse. I forgot the damn phone on the bed.

With a resounding sigh, I place the cord back on my stand and grip the mattress. I'm about to pull myself up when I hear the floor in front of my bathroom creak.

There's only one spot in this whole damn apartment that creaks and it's the spot right in front of my bathroom.

Which is right next to my bedroom.

Trying my best to stay calm, I release the mattress and scoot myself under the bed. I take one last deep breath to calm my racing heart and force myself to take calm, steady, quiet, breaths.

It's only seconds later when I hear footsteps enter my room. I loved this apartment because it didn't have carpet. It's so much easier to move around in my chair when I don't have to deal with the carpet.

So, I hear each step the person takes as they walk across the hardwood floor.

It's not Sammy. There's no way that he would scare me like this. It's not Laura, because she's in lockdown. And it's not my sister, Becky, because she went to Florida on vacation. Even if she was back, she doesn't live anywhere near me.

Not to mention these footfalls sound too heavy to belong to a woman.

"I know you're in here, Dove," a heavily accented voice says. "You don't know who I am," the man continues. "And until yesterday, I had no idea who you were. But I'm glad Ink finally got himself a woman. I was starting to worry about him when I learned everyone else had settled down."

My breathing sounds too loud. Can he hear me? Does he really know I'm here?

"I'm here to teach the Sons a lesson," the man says, sitting on my bed.

He definitely knows I'm here.

"I knew that the pussies would lock themselves inside their clubhouse sooner or later. I just didn't think it would be so soon. Do you know what they did to me?"

I hold my breath and wait for him to continue. Maybe he'll just talk and then leave.

"The details don't matter much," he says. He definitely has an accent, but I can't tell where it's from. "Just know that they destroyed my life and I'm here to repay the debt. Because of them, my life has been ruined. My father disowns me, and I will do anything to get back in his favor."

Already knowing that he knows I'm here, I ask shakily, "What does any of that have to do with me?"

The man laughs and it's probably the most horrible thing I've ever heard.

"Well, Dove," he says. "I'm glad you asked. I need that club to pay for what they did. I want to watch the life drain from each and every single member's eyes. But not before I fuck their women next to their broken bodies as they watch helplessly."

Horrid, horrid man.

"I can't get inside that club just yet, so I'll settle for the next best thing. Ink's woman."

My first reaction is to deny that I'm Sammy's woman. But I know I am. Sammy knows I am. And, apparently, this man does as well.

The man suddenly appears under the bed and he grabs my arms and pulls. I try my best to pull away, I have strong upper-body strength and give the man a hard time, but it's all I can do. I can yank, twist, and turn to get him to let go but where do I go from there?

My chair is on the other side of the bed. I can't just get up and run. No matter how much I fight, he's going to win.

But I don't care. I keep yanking and biting, twisting, turning, and punching. In the end, as I knew, he won. But, not without a few battle wounds. Once my strength is gone, he tosses me on the bed.

"I'm impressed, Dove," the man smiles through a bloodied and swollen lip. "I was expecting this to be easy but I'm happy to learn that you're a fighter."

"Come a little closer," I dare. "I still have a little fight left."

I casually reach near my pillow where I dropped my phone. Once I feel it, I grasp it tightly. I may not be able to call anyone, but I can sure give this dick a broken nose if I hit him with it hard enough.

"I don't doubt it a bit, Dove," he says. "But I have other plans."

Just then, two other men walk into my room. They both have the same black hair, dark eyes, and wide nose that the first man has. They all look related.

"These are my cousins," the man says. "Antonio and Frankie."

"And you are?" I ask because he still hasn't given me his name.

"You'll learn who I am before I leave," he says with a sinister smile. "Boys, do your worst."

I watch with dread as the man leans against the wall and Antonio and Frankie make their way towards me.

I try to calm my racing heart but it's of no use. I'm about to be beaten or raped. Possibly both and there isn't a damn thing I can do about it.

I scream as loud as I can hoping one of my neighbors hears me, but I know it's hopeless. We've heard screams in this apartment complex before and all that my neighbors do is poke their noses against the window while I call the police.

I squeeze my eyes shut as one of the men slams a hand against my mouth. I don't dare open my eyes as my pajamas are ripped off and a rough hand squeezes my breast. I feel another hand cup my most private area and I let the tears fall.

I use every bit of strength I have to fight back. I move my upper body from side to side, I continue to hit something with the phone. But it's no use.

I don't stop fighting even though I know I won't win. I can see Sammy behind my eyes screaming at me to not give up. I can feel his love encouraging me to stay strong. I can hear him tell me that I'll make it through this.

I lay there, hands held above my head and a heavy body on my chest as the other man rapes me.

It seems to last for hours. But eventually, it stops. The weight on my chest leaves and the man between my legs leaves.

"Now, now, Dove," the man says. My eyes are still shut tightly as I feel him sit on the bed beside me.

Using a gentle touch that I didn't know evil possessed, he moves the hair off my face and wipes away the tears. I don't dare move.

"It wasn't all that bad, was it?" he says.

I slowly open my eyes and look at the man.

"So much strength behind those eyes," he says. "Ink is lucky to have you, Dove. It's a shame that I'm going to have to kill him."

He stands and walks to my chair on the other side of the bed. I watch as he slowly unlocks the wheels and moves my only source of mobility to the other side of the room. Well out of reach.

"Who are you?" I ask, my voice rough.

He looks back and smiles a smile that I'll have nightmares about for years.

"Sweet, sweet Dove," he says in his heavy accent. "Why, I'm Roman Hernández, of course."

Then he turns and leaves, his maniacal laughter following behind him.

I don't move until I know they're out of my apartment. When I'm sure that I'm finally alone, I lose it. Tears fall from my eyes in rivers that I can't contain. My body hurts, I feel nasty and I want to take a shower. But, even more, I want Sammy.

The thought of Sammy makes me cry harder. I had doubt that he would want me because of my legs, now I know he won't want me because I'm nasty. I'll never get their touch off of me.

I'm not sure how long I lay in bed crying before I finally pull myself together. I need to think rationally even though I'm scared and only want to curl in a ball and die.

I don't know if the man who raped me wore a condom, so I need to get to the hospital. Luckily, the man I was hitting with my phone simply plucked it from my hands and placed it on the bed.

I feel as if I'm not really present as I plug the phone in, power it up, and dial 911.

"911, what's your emergency?"

"My name is Rachel Justice," I hear myself distantly say. "I live at the apartment complex on Washington, apartment thirty-four B. I was just raped."

"Rachel," the dispatcher says. "Is your attacker still in your home?"

"No, I don't think so."

"Can you go and lock your door?"

"I'm a paraplegic," I explain. "And my chair is too far away."

"That's alright, Rachel. Can you tell me where you're at in your apartment?"

"I'm in my bedroom on my bed," I answer. "Please hurry."

I hang up the phone and lay back down. Knowing that people will be crowded in my room, I take the blanket from the other side of the bed and drape it over my now naked body.

Why can't I feel anything? I know I'm scared and in pain. My body is shaking, and my heart is racing. But I just lay here waiting for the paramedics to arrive.

CHAPTER ELEVEN
Ink

It's three in the morning and I can't fall asleep. I head downstairs and see what we have to snack on.

"I guess I wasn't the only one unable to sleep," I say when I see Wolf, Slim, Bear, Bella, and Laura all sitting on the sofas.

"Must be in the air," Wolf says.

I walk over and take an empty seat next to Bella.

"Talking about anything interesting?" I ask.

"Just about the children," Bella says. "Laura is concerned about how these lockdowns will affect their emotional well-being."

"They seem to be handling it well," I say. "Luckily we haven't had many lockdowns and hopefully we won't have anymore. But the children seem to actually enjoy them."

"Because they don't have to go to school," Laura says, laughing. "But I think you're right. They seem to be fine."

I lean back in my chair and look around.

"I thought we had a tv in here," I say.

"We did," Slim answers. "But I needed one more screen to hook my system to. So, it's in Bear's office temporarily."

I'm about to give Slim a lecture on taking the only

source of entertainment we have during this lockdown when someone's phone rings.

"That's me," Laura says, reaching for her phone on the table beside her seat. "Who would be calling at this time of night?"

"Hello," she answers. "This is her. May I ask whose calling?"

We all wait in anticipation as she listens to the caller on the other line.

I smile. We are a nosey bunch.

"What?" Laura whispers.

The worry in her voice has us all interested for a different reason.

"Oh, god, no," she says, tears filling her eyes. "Yeah, I'll be right there."

Laura hangs up the phone and dread fills me when she looks right in my eyes.

"Rachel was attacked," she says and my heart stops. "She's at the hospital but they say that she's going to be physically fine."

I can't speak. I can't move. I can't fucking breathe.

"Physically?" Slim asks the question on my mind. "What about mentally?"

The tears that were pooling in Laura's eyes fall.

"I'm not sure," she admits shakily. "She was raped."

A sound I've never heard before rips out of my body as I stand and race for my room.

"Ink," someone yells.

But I don't give a fuck. Nothing matters now except getting to my woman's side. I grab my keys and run back down the stairs. Before I get to the exit, I'm grabbed from behind.

"Brother, you need to take a deep breath and center

yourself before you get on that bike."

"Trigger, if you don't release me in the next three seconds, I'm going to rip your fucking arms off," I say as calmly as possible.

"Think rationally, brother," Bear says, coming to stand in front of me. "You have one of the fastest bikes out there. If you get on that beast with a clouded mind, you'll end up killing yourself before you have a chance to kill the person who hurt your woman."

"RAPED!" I scream. "YOU MEAN THE PERSON WHO FUCKING RAPED MY WOMAN!"

I can't contain the anger no matter how hard I try, but I know they're right. I close my eyes and take as many deep breaths as I need until my heart slows to a normal pace.

"Trigger, Wolf," Bear says. "I want you two with him. Laura, I need you to stay here."

"Oh, fuck no," she says. "Rachel is my girl, and she needs me. So, fuck you for telling me to stay put. You ain't my daddy."

"That's my sis," I hear Chains laugh. "Gets her spunk from her big brother."

Trigger finally releases me and I turn to look at the room. Everyone is awake and watching.

"Ink," Thea says.

Thea doesn't talk much, but when she does, she has a calming voice that can soothe even the meanest man. Which explains how she deals with Trigger.

"Please be careful on your way to the hospital," she says. "When you get there, be patient with her because she's going to be scared."

I nod and pull Thea into a hug. I hold her a few seconds longer than normal before letting her go.

"Laura, stay here," I say. "I need you well rested because

tomorrow you need to be with her while I go fucking hunting."

Laura wants to say something, but she nods her agreement.

Turning, I walk out of the building and to my bike.

"We'll follow," I hear Wolf say.

I start my bike and race towards the hospital.

Towards the woman holding my heart.

Rachel

"Almost done, honey."

I'm lying on a hospital bed while one nurse holds my knees apart and another takes swabs of my vagina.

I've been here for over an hour while these women perform a rape kit. They've combed out my hair, they've swabbed multiple parts of my body, they've taken blood work, pictures, cleaned under my nails but what they haven't allowed me to do is take a freaking shower.

I know the nurses are just trying to help but all I can think about as their hands roam my body are the males who did the same thing but for different reasons.

It's messed up when a person goes to a hospital because they were raped only to have to deal with such an invasive procedure. I now understand why some people never say a word. If I would have known I had to go through all of this, I probably wouldn't have called them.

"We couldn't reach your sister," the nurse holding my knees says. "So, we called your friend, Laura, instead. She said she was on her way."

I nod at the nurse and go back to trying my best to ignore the tickling sensation of the swabs between my legs.

I'm glad that they couldn't get ahold of my sister. If I would have actually spoken up when they asked, I could have told them to call Laura instead. But, for some reason, I haven't been able to bring myself to say a single word since hanging up the phone with the emergency dispatcher.

Luckily, Laura is my second emergency contact after Becky.

Finally, after what seems like hours, all the testing is complete.

"These are the pills I told you about when you first arrived," a nurse says. "One is a morning-after pill to prevent pregnancy and the other is prophylaxis to prevent any sexually transmitted infections."

I already signed the consent form for the drugs and rape kit before they started so I take the small cup and dump the medication into my mouth and swallow.

I accept the water she holds out and drink until the pills are fully down.

The nurse told me her name twice already, but I can't seem to remember it. I keep repeating over and over in my head the three names I don't ever want to forget.

Antonio, Frankie, and Roman Hernández.

The police stop by and ask me questions, but I just shake my head. I don't want to talk to the police. I don't want to talk to the nurse. I just want a scolding hot shower and I want to forget.

But more than anything else, I want revenge. And that isn't something the police can help me with.

"It's best if we interview you now, Miss Justice," the police officer kindly says. "When the details are fresh in your mind."

I look at the officer and mentally will him to leave.

I'll never forget a single detail of what happened to me tonight. But talking to this man is the last thing I want to do. He can't help me.

"Alright," he sighs. "How about me and my partner come to your place tomorrow to go over the details? She's on her way now but we can wait until morning."

I nod my head and close my eyes. I know he used the pronoun 'she' on purpose and I'm thankful for it. For all the bravado I want to feel, being alone with a strange male isn't something I'm able to deal with right now.

The officer leaves and I'm finally left alone.

I drift off to a light sleep full of nightmares and sinister smiles.

CHAPTER TWELVE
Ink

I've been standing in the doorway to Rachel's room just watching her sleep. I wouldn't call it a restful sleep, but I'm half afraid to wake her up.

What if she doesn't want me here? What if seeing another man only trigger's things for her and makes it worse?

Maybe I should have had Laura come after all.

"Can I help you?"

I turn around and come face to face with a female nurse.

"How long has she been asleep?" I ask.

"Who are you?" She asks firmly.

I have to give it to the woman, she's a bit scary.

"I'm Rachel's man," I say with determination. "When can I take her home?"

"Well, Rachel's man," she says. "I'm nurse Wing and Rachel is under my care while she's in this building. Until she is awake and gives the okay for you to take her out, she stays put."

I don't hit women!!!

How many times in a week am I going to have to remind myself this?

"Listen here," I start.

"Sammy."

The sound of Rachel's voice pulls me from the difficult nurse, and I spin around and rush to her side.

"Baby," I whisper as I lean down and kiss her forehead. "I'm so fucking sorry I wasn't there to protect you."

I'll never forgive myself. I left her alone knowing that shit was going down with the club. I don't know who did this to her, but I have a feeling it has to do with the Sons.

"Please, take me out of here, Sammy," Rachel says.

I lean back to get a good look at her face and my heart stops at the pure anguish I see in her eyes.

"Alright baby," I say, not even attempting to stop my eyes from misting over. "Alright."

I look around for her chair and turn to face the nurse still standing by the door.

"You left her in here alone with no way to leave?" I say, my anger at its peak.

The nurse's hard demeanor changed to one of confusion.

"She didn't come in with a chair," she tells me. "She actually hasn't spoken a single word since she got here. Not until you showed up."

"Give me the address brother," Wolf says. "I'll go grab her chair and anything else she needs."

I nod my thanks and give him her address.

"I'll meet you there," Wolf says to Trigger. "I'm going to go switch my bike with my truck."

I pick Rachel up and cradle her to my chest. I'm never fucking letting her out of my sight again.

"Just grab her some clothes and her bathroom shit," I tell them. "Anything else she needs I'll just go buy."

"Do you have any medications you need me to get, sweetheart?" Wolf asks.

Rachel shakes her head against my chest, and I relay her message.

I'm on my way outside, Rachel still tucked tightly against my chest, when I remember that I rode here on my fucking bike.

Damnit.

"Already taken care of," Trigger says. "Bear's outside waiting for your bike keys."

I head outside to where I parked my bike and see Bear standing next to it.

"Here's my car, brother," he says. "I'll take your bike back."

Not able to speak, I nod and place Rachel in the passenger seat of Bear's car and buckle her in.

"Don't forget that she's got power," I say, handing my keys to Bear. "Don't have too much fun and get yourself hurt or Rose will kill me."

Bear laughs and straddles my bike.

"See you at home," he says, starting my bike and driving away.

I get into the car and turn to face my woman.

"I'll never be able to forgive myself," I admit. "This happened because of me."

Rachel wipes her eyes before facing me.

"Don't you dare blame yourself," she says, fire in her eyes. "The men who did this knew exactly what it would do to you. They know exactly what to do to hit your club hard. It was hard and I was so scared, but I never once blamed you.

However, I did pay attention, Sammy. I paid attention to everything said to me. Every sound, every smell, and every name. And, I didn't say a single word to the police."

I'm shocked at the hardness in her voice.

"Why didn't you talk to the police?" I ask.

Rachel turns to look out the side window.

"Because they wouldn't have done a damn thing," she says. "And because when you find them, and you will, Sammy, I want to look all three men in the eyes when they take their last breath."

What the fuck did she say?

"Did you say, three men?" I ask quietly.

Rachel finally turns back to face me with a small smile on her face. A smile of pure ultimate satisfaction.

"I know their names, Sammy," she whispers, ignoring my question. "The idiot told me all of their names. And I made sure I didn't forget."

I know Rachel will always remember how she felt when she was attacked. I know that she'll have nightmares for many years to come. I know that she'll always have that small fear of it happening again.

But my woman is strong as fuck. She won't let this break her. She's going to be the reason I break the fuckers who attacked her. And she knows it.

"That's my girl," I say, smiling. "So fucking strong. It makes me love you even more."

I start the car and pull out of the lot. But not before I watched Rachel's eyes widen, her face blush and her smile deepen.

Yeah, my woman won't let this break her.

CHAPTER THIRTEEN
Rachel

I'm angry.

No, I'm beyond angry. I'm infuriated. Freaking livid.

I'm murderously seething with rage.

I don't like the feelings running through my body but at the same time, it's helping me cope.

All I can think about is revenge.

Antonio, Frankie, and Roman.
Antonio, Frankie, and Roman.
Antonio, Frankie, and Roman.

I'm not sure if it was Frankie or Antonio who raped me, but it doesn't matter. And, as strange as it sounds, I feel most of my anger towards the first man. Roman.

"I want more than anything to hear what you're thinking about, baby," Sammy says after ten minutes of driving silently. "But only when you're ready."

"Is there a shower and hot water at your clubhouse?" I ask.

Sammy nods his head.

"The first thing I want to do is shower and scrub my body until I feel as clean as I can," I admit. "Then I'm going to need your help, Sammy."

"Anything, love," he says. "Absolutely anything."

"I'll go through the details of what happened with you

and your brothers," I say. "I'll tell you every single thing that was said to me. Then I want you to promise me that you will find these men and that you will give me the revenge that I so desperately crave."

Sammy is quiet as he pulls into a parking lot full of bikes. He shuts off the car and turns towards me.

"You have my word that these fuckers will pay for what they did."

That's not exactly what I asked but looking into his eyes I see a rage matching my own looking back at me.

"Thank you," I whisper.

Sammy brings his hand to my face and cups my chin.

"I love you, baby. I hope to god you know that."

Tears fall from my eyes for an entirely different reason.

"I love you, too, Sammy," I admit. "I have for a very long time."

Sammy gently smiles before releasing my face and exiting the car. He opens my door seconds later, unbuckles me, and picks me up as if I weigh nothing.

"Wolf and Trigger will be here soon with your chair," he says, walking towards a large building. "Should be here by the time you get out of the shower."

My only thought at the moment is that shower. I don't care about anything else.

"You most likely don't have a shower chair, do you?" I ask, already knowing the answer.

"Believe it or not, we do," a new voice says.

I turn my head to see a hulking man with a large beard walking towards us.

"Prez," Sammy greets. "Trig and Wolf should be here soon."

"I know," he answers. This must be Bear. "My wife was attacked a couple of years back and her leg was broken," he says, looking at me. "Every now and again, it acts up on her and she has a hard time standing. So, we have a shower chair here and at home for when she needs them. You're more than welcome to use it anytime you need to."

I smile at the kind man before tucking my face against Sammy's chest.

"Please take me to a shower," I whisper desperately.

I tune out anything else said as I focus on Sammy's warmth and scent. The need to shower is all-consuming. I feel dirty. Beyond dirty. I can't think of a way to explain how filthy I feel. But I know that it's going to take a long time before I finally feel clean.

I feel the rumble of Sammy's chest as he talks, and I simply squeeze my eyes shut and recall the faces of the three men.

Antonio, Frankie, Roman.

"I'm going to put you in this chair, Rachel," Sammy says, bringing me out of my head. "Then go get Laura."

I jerk my head back in shock.

"Please, don't leave," I beg. "Please, don't leave me alone."

I don't want to sound weak, but at this moment, I feel weak. And I feel safe to feel weak as long as Sammy is with me.

"Alright, baby," he says. "Do you need help getting this off?"

I glance down, only now noticing that I'm still wearing a hospital gown.

I nod my head and hope that he doesn't expect that this will go any further tonight. I'm not ready for that just yet but I don't think I can do this alone.

"Alright," he says softly, placing me on the chair inside

the walk-in shower.

Without another word, he unties the two gowns on either side of my body and lifts me off the seat to completely remove them.

"Mother fuckers," Sammy says.

I follow his gaze down to the large finger-shaped bruises on both of my hips.

Sammy's eyes roam up from my hips in a slow caress as he takes in the rest of me. It's not done in a sexual way. If anything, the look of murder in his eyes the whole time takes any playfulness away.

I look away as his eyes near my breasts knowing what he'll find.

"I'm going to fucking kill them," he growls. "Slowly."

I watch his hand reach forward and I shake my head.

"Please, don't touch it," I beg. "I'm so dirty, Sammy. Please, don't let it get on you any more than it already has when you held me."

The storm in his eyes grows with intensity as he pulls back. He doesn't say anything as he starts the water. The feeling of water drifting down my skin is a relief, but it isn't enough.

"Soap," I beg.

I take the washcloth Sammy holds out and squeeze a large amount of someone's body wash. I scrub my body until it's raw but it's not working. Leaning forward, I turn the cold water down until all I feel is hot.

I watch as my skin turns red from the water and rawer from scrubbing. But it's still not working. I still feel dirty.

My tears are falling full force, mingling with the hot water cascading down my face. I lean forward and turn the cold water completely off.

The scalding water burns my skin, but I need more.

Squeezing more soap on my cloth, I scrub between my legs until the only thing I feel is pain.

And still, the dirty feeling remains.

I scream in frustration at the unfairness of my life. I'm a good person. Why did this happen to me? What did I do to deserve something so horrible?

I lean forward in resignation as the hot water engulfs my back.

I stay in this position and cry until the water runs cold. Then I lean back and let the cold water sting my skin in the hopes of it helping clean me.

I'm not sure how long I just sit here when the water turns off and I glance up to see Sammy watching me with such sadness. I watch as the tears fall freely down his face and land on the floor.

"Baby," he says roughly. "Let me help you."

I shake my head.

"It's no use, Sammy," I cry. "I'm dirty. I'll never feel clean again."

Sammy reaches for a towel and gently dry's my face.

"You're not dirty," he says. "And the type of clean you need isn't something that we can fix with soap and water. If you can trust me, sweetheart, then, with time, I'll make you feel clean again."

I want to doubt what he says but I'm so desperate that I need to know how.

"How?" I ask

"With love, baby," he says, kissing my forehead. "With love and with care. Now, let's get you dried off and dressed."

I sit patiently as he dries off my body and realize that Sammy's touch and his words are already working better than soap and water. I focus on his touch as he pulls off his shirt and helps me into it.

I smile against his neck as he lifts me, making sure his shirt is tucked beneath my butt.

"Thank you," I whisper.

He doesn't respond with words, but his arms holding me tighter against his body and the soft kiss to the top of the head tell me all I need to know.

Sammy has me and he isn't letting go.

Ink

I have never, in my entire life, felt rage course through my body like it's doing right now. It's taking every ounce of self-control I have to stay calm around my woman. I don't want her stressed out or scared any more than she already is.

Watching her scrub her body raw in the shower was heartbreaking. I wanted more than anything to jump in and help her. But she would have refused my touch at that time.

I hate that she feels dirty. When I get my hands on the fuckers who raped her, I plan to take my time making them pay.

"Sammy," Rachel says against my neck. "You're going to hurt your back carrying me around everywhere. Find me a chair and plop my butt down on it."

"Plop her over here next to me," Laura says as I enter the lounge room.

Letting her go is the last thing I want to do, but I really need to talk to Bear.

"You okay with that, baby?" I ask Rachel.

She hesitates for a second before nodding her head.

I walk over and put Rachel on the couch next to Laura. I take a step back and watch as they both start crying and hugging each other. I turn and head to Bear's office.

"Trigger and Wolf just pulled in," Slim says as I enter the office.

"Can you have them take everything up to my room?" I ask him. "Except her chair."

"Sure thing," Slim says, leaving the room.

"Prez, I think we need to call a meeting with Rachel," I tell Bear whose looking over something on his computer.

"Why?" he asks.

It's a legitimate question but it pisses me the fuck off. I take a deep breath in to control this rage. I need to find the men who hurt her.

"She has names," is all I say.

Hawk looks up from Slim's security consoles with wide eyes.

"She has names?" he asks. "The man who attacked her?"

"Men," I correct. "The men who attacked her. And yes."

"Five minutes," Bear says. "I'm texting everyone now."

With a nod, I leave and head back to Rachel.

I need these names more than I need my next breath.

CHAPTER FOURTEEN
Rachel

"Then he turns back and tells me his name before leaving."

I needed to tell her. Laura has been my best friend for years and I needed her to know what happened to me. I know that I'm about to tell Sammy and all of his brothers, but I need my girl to know, too.

"I'm so sorry that I wasn't there for you," Laura cries. "I should have freaking known that you would have been targeted since you knew both me and Ink. It was careless not to realize that."

I smile and gently elbow her arm.

"If I remember correctly," I say, trying to hold back my own tears. "I was pretty adamant about being completely fine out there on my own."

Laura doesn't say anything. I can understand how she might think this is her fault, but I truly don't blame her, Sammy, or anyone else.

"I have something for you, Miss Rachel."

I look up at the voice and freeze.

Laura chuckles.

"That's Wolf," she whispers. "He's new. And so very sexy."

"Thank you for the compliment, Miss Laura," Wolf grins, pushing my chair next to me. "You're both very beautiful young women."

I grin up at Wolf.

"You have manners," I say.

He simply smiles and nods.

"Can you give Sammy lessons?" I ask, trying to hold my giggle in. "He's about as rude and obnoxious as they come."

"I'll have you know, baby, that it took years and years to hone my craft, I think I'll skip on those lessons."

For the first time since my attack, I laugh. Sammy walks up behind Wolf and pats him on the shoulder. They walk off talking as I'm still working through my giggles.

"That man is a fruit loop," Laura says.

I nod my head in agreement.

I watch as Sammy and Wolf talk. I can't move my eyes away from him. In high school, he was the hottest boy around. Every girl wanted him, and every boy wanted to be him. I always had a crush on the popular boy with the muscles and tanned skin.

But, looking at him now, what I thought was hot back then is nothing compared to what he looks like now. The boyish good looks have all but disappeared and standing there now is pure unadulterated male. His muscles now are out of this world and his tanned skin glistens from the light shining through the window. His eyes hold stories, but one thing remains the same, the beautiful green color that seems to shine brighter than the sun. I've always loved his eyes.

"I see why they call him Ink now," Laura says.

Oh, yeah, the tattoos. They are everywhere. I haven't let myself fully examine them for fear of being caught, but Sammy has tattoos up both of his arms, across his chest, over his shoulders, and down his back.

Shirtless Sammy is bad news.

Shoot, fully clothed Sammy is bad news.

"Did you hear me, babe?"

Startled, I look up and glare.

"You need to put a shirt on," I say.

"You're wearing my shirt," Sammy grins.

"Is this the only one you own?" I tease.

"It's my Friday shirt," he smirks. "I can't wear any other shirt today except that one."

"Today's Tuesday," Wolf says causing us all to laugh.

"You're all just jealous that you don't look this good."

"Dear God, shut up," I laugh. The man's ego sure hasn't changed any.

"Don't you dare start that shit, too," Sammy says.

I don't understand why everyone is in tears with their laughter, but I smile and remind myself to ask Laura later on what was so funny.

"You ready for this?" Sammy asks once everyone has calmed down.

I know what he's talking about. I want to say no. I want to stay right here in this little bubble of smiles and laughter.

But, even more than that, I truly do want revenge. So, with a reluctant determination, I nod my head.

Sammy places me in my chair, and I shift around until I get comfortable.

"What are these buckles for?" he asks.

I warm at his curiosity.

"While I do have most muscle control in my lower back, it's not always the strongest," I admit. "Sometimes, I need that belt to help hold me in my chair."

"And these?"

I look down to see him touch the wheel locks.

"It locks my wheels in place, so my chair doesn't move when I don't want it to."

His eyes roam my chair with an intense curiosity.

"Wouldn't an electric chair be better?" Someone asks.

I look over at the voice and it's a woman I haven't yet met.

"Sorry, I'm Thea," she says, blushing.

"Nice to meet you, Thea," I smile. "And yes, I'm sure an electric chair would be easier for certain things, but I prefer the mobility of the one I have. Those power chairs are bulky and heavy and don't move the way this one does."

"We best head in now," the man beside Thea says. "Go save my boy from that insane woman."

Thea laughs. "Brendon is fine with Bella," she says. "Ignore all of his facial expressions," she tells me. "He's not as grumpy or as mean as he wants people to think he is."

I'll have to take her word for it. Because the man looks pissed off just standing there. Well, until he looks down at Thea. Then a soft, almost non-existent, smile appears on his face.

"Let's go, baby."

I turn my chair and follow Sammy. My heart is beating a thousand beats per second knowing that I'm about to relive that whole situation again. One that I'm sure will be in my dreams for years to come.

Ink

I'm pacing back and forth as Rachel tells us everything that happened. She's being so brave and I'm beyond proud of her. But I'm about to fucking lose it.

I held her hand as she walked us through her attack and was surprised as fuck that I didn't lose it sooner. She's in the middle of explaining how she had to fall off of her bed to get to her phone charger when she stops talking.

Looking back, I watch as tears slowly flow down her face. I memorize the pain and the fear in her eyes. I want that image in my mind when I fucking kill the bastards who did this.

"Go back to before you called the police," Bear says softly. "You told us that the two men who held you down and attacked you left while the first man stayed behind. What happened after that?"

I push my own feelings aside and sit down next to my woman. My arms ache to grab her out of her chair and hold her but I think she needs her personal space while she tells us what happened.

If it was up to me, I would never let her out of my arms again.

"I opened my eyes," she whispers. "And he was sitting on the side of my bed gently moving the hair off of my forehead. I remember thinking that it was so odd that something so evil could be so gentle."

Dead. I don't care who the fuck he is. He's dead.

Rachel

As strange as it is to say, telling this group of rough-looking men about my attack isn't so hard. Going over every single detail multiple times is making my heart race and the fear return, but I don't feel embarrassed or scared to tell them.

Maybe it's because I know deep down that they're all good men.

I watch as Sammy paces the room and I feel bad for being the cause of his anger. Rationally, I know that he isn't mad at me, but I do know that I'm the reason his emotions are all over the place. It takes him a few minutes, but he finally sits back down beside me.

"He told me that he wanted to teach you all a lesson," I continue. "He said that this club ruined his life."

"Do you know who he is?" Bear asks me.

I shake my head.

"I've never met him or the other two males before today," I admit.

I watch the look of disappointment cross the men's faces.

"But, for some odd reason," I continue. "He did tell me their names."

"Do you remember them?" The largest male asks. I think his name is Brick.

Antonia, Frankie, Roman. I'll never forget them for the rest of my days.

I look down at my hands and nod. I already told Sammy that I knew the names, but it's clear he didn't let everyone else know that I did. Except the two men, Bear and Hawk. They don't look surprised at my admission.

"The two men who attacked me," I said, not yet able to say the word rape to them. "The first man called them Antonio and Frankie. But I'm not sure which one was which."

"Did he happen to give any last names?" Slim asks.

He's been sitting beside me typing away on his laptop. There's no telling what he's digging through.

I nod.

"The first man told me that they were cousins of his," I say.

"And what was the first man's name, baby?"

I look over and watch as Sammy's green eyes lock onto mine. I keep that connection as I continue.

"Roman Hernández," I say.

I watch in fascination as Sammy's eyes widen and darken.

"WHAT?"

"No, fucking way."

"He said that this club ruined his life," I continue, ignoring everyone's outbursts. "Apparently his father disowned him, and he thinks getting revenge against you for whatever you did will put him back in his father's good graces."

"He's supposed to be in prison," Chains says.

"Yeah, not so much," Slim says from beside me. "It appears that the prison had a power failure last month and half a dozen convicts escaped. Including, our one and only, Roman Hernández and his father."

"I should have killed that fucker when I had the chance," Bear growls.

"Wait a second," Sammy says. "The signature from the notes."

"H.C. Hernández Cartel," Trigger finishes.

"Increase security," Bear says. "Bring in the fucking Bunnies if you have to. I want someone on watch twenty-four seven."

"I don't think the Bunnies are all that necessary," Sammy says guiltily.

I simply shake my head and grin.

"You're a manslut through and through," I say, causing everyone to chuckle.

"Not anymore, baby," Sammy says seriously. "You're all I want."

I look down at my hands, hiding my smile.

What those men did to me scared me, hurt me, and humiliated me. But it didn't break me. It didn't take away my desire for Sammy. If anything, it made me crave him more. Because I know that he'll make the feeling of those touching me vanish.

I just hope that he's still actually interested in me knowing that I've been dirtied up by his enemy.

CHAPTER FIFTEEN
Ink

Roman fucking Hernández.

The bastard escaped prison and decided to enact his revenge by having my woman raped?

I'm itching to get my hands on all three of them.

I take Rachel back out to the lounge to hang with Laura. We have plans to make and she doesn't need to be involved in that part.

"What's wrong with Rose?" Laura asks as we stop by the couch.

Looking over I see Rose engulfed in Bear's arms as she trembles in fear.

"Roman Hernández escaped," I tell Laura.

Her eyes widen with understanding.

"What am I missing?" Rachel asks.

"I'll tell you all about it," Laura says.

"We both will," Rose adds, sitting down next to Laura. "It's a long story."

"I need to head back," I tell Rachel. "Will you be alright?"

She nods with confidence. I smile and lean down to press a light kiss to her perfect lips. I'm not sure when she's going to be ready for me in all ways, but I'll wait a lifetime if I have to.

For now, a small peck to show her that I care.

"I do love you," I whisper against her lips. "I was a fool to let you go all those years ago. It's never going to happen again."

I kiss away the single tear under her eye and walk away before I completely embarrass myself in front of all of the ladies.

"Who's the pansy now?" Chains says when I walk back into the meeting room.

"Fucker," I smile. "Turns out, being a pansy isn't all that bad."

"How the hell are we going to find Hernández?" Bear asks.

"Well, we can mark off his father's place," Brick says.

"I want him found," Bear growls. "That man thinks he owns my wife."

"Do you think that he'll come after her again?" Slim asks.

I nod my head. "Based off of the notes he left behind and what he told and done to Rachel, he's planning on using the women against us."

"You still believe that our partners make us weak?" Hawk asks.

I remember saying that. Hell, I remember thinking it. It feels like a lifetime ago, not just a couple of weeks.

"Not weak," I admit. "Because knowing that my woman was attacked is making me feel anything but weak. I will destroy this whole fucking world to make her feel safe again."

Everyone nods their understanding.

"Let's start with the Hernández Cartel," Trigger says. "And this time, no fucking cops."

"Amen," Slim says. "I'm with the bloodthirsty man this

time around."

"What? Don't you miss Detective Dick?" Chains teases.

I smile, despite the anger rolling through me. If I never see Detective Dick again, I will die a happy man.

"Alright," Slim says. "Let me do some digging. I might not be able to pinpoint where Roman is, but I might be able to locate his two cousins."

"That's a start," Bear says. "As soon as you do, let us know. I know I want to get my hands on the fuckers who hurt one of our sisters."

"Fuck yeah!"

I nod my gratitude at their acceptance and stand.

"I'm going to go take Rachel upstairs to bed," I say. "Wake me up when it's my turn on security."

Without another word, I leave the room.

I'm fucking exhausted and can only imagine how my woman is feeling.

I find her right where I left her, only she's in tears and hugging Rose.

"You've had such a horrible life," Rachel says. "I'm so sorry."

"Don't be," Rose tells her. "Because it led me to where I am today and that isn't something that I ever want to be changed."

"Life is so unfair sometimes," Rachel says. She hasn't noticed me yet, so I keep quiet. "But the bad things that happen to us only make us stronger. And I know that if I hadn't been in the accident that lost me my legs, then I wouldn't have the strength to go through what happened to me today."

"You two are killing me," Laura says, wiping her face.

Rose laughs and pats Laura's knee.

"Look at us, crying like a bunch of women," Rose jokes.

"We're sisters, and together, with our men, we're strong. And nothing can break us."

"That's right, bitches," Slim says, flopping down between Laura and Rose. "Just remember, if you get buried alive, don't panic. It depletes your oxygen much faster. Lesson learned the hard way."

"Wait, what?" Rachel asks, shocked.

"Well, you see…"

"Storytime over," Hawk says. "Come on, sweet boy, let's go get you something to eat before you glue yourself to that system of yours."

"Fine, big guy," Slim says. "Let's pencil storytime in when this shit is over with."

With a shake of my head, I walk over to Rachel.

"You sleepy, baby?" I ask.

"Exhausted," she admits.

We tell everyone goodnight and make our way to the stairs.

"Small problem," Rachel says. "My legs don't appear to be working."

I chuckle at her joke and lean down.

"You are something else," I say. "Arms around my neck."

I lift her and make our way to my room.

Rachel

Sammy sits me down on a full-sized bed. I start to scoot back towards the pillow when a thought occurs to me.

"Just how many women have you had sex with on this bed?" I ask.

Sammy cocks his eyebrow. "Do you really want to know the answer to that question?"

"Not really," I admit softly.

I hate knowing that he's slept with so many people. But that's just something I'm going to have to work on. Well, if he still wants to be with me.

"I haven't slept with a woman in this bed for many months now," he admits. "And the bedding has been changed multiple times since then."

I smile. I love how he's trying his best to make me feel comfortable.

"What are you thinking about so hard?" he asks.

My first instinct is to lie. But nothing ever gets resolved by lying.

"I'll understand if you've changed your mind about what you said before," I say quietly. "I wouldn't blame you if you walked away."

"What the fuck are you talking about?" he asks. "I'm not going anywhere, baby. Why would you even think that? I thought you agreed to give us a chance."

"I did," I admit, trying my best to hold back my tears. "But I've been violated in the worst way possible. Why would anybody want to be with me after what happened?"

Sammy lays me down and pulls me against his body.

"I'm never letting you go, again," he says against the top of my head. "I'm right here, baby, and I'm not going anywhere. I love you and I don't care if we spend the rest of our lives falling asleep just like this."

I snuggle my head further against his chest.

"I love you, too, Sammy," I say, rubbing the smooth skin of his naked chest. "I'm just so scared that I won't be enough when I am ready."

"You're more than enough," he says.

I smile and lean my head back.

"You're the only person I've ever willingly had sex with," I admit, ignoring the burning on my face and the fear in my heart. "I had no idea what I was doing then, and I have no idea what I'm doing now."

Sammy pushes my head back against his chest. He's trying to hide his emotions, but I saw both the anger and the desire in his eyes.

I'm just as conflicted. I'm scared over what happened and worried something's wrong with me because I do feel desire for Sammy when it feels like I shouldn't right now.

"As for your legs," he says, interrupting my thoughts. "I've done my research and when the time is right and you feel ready, we are going to have one hell of a night."

I feel the burn in my face.

"Just one night?" I tease.

"Every night," he says. "Now sleep, baby. I need to be up soon."

I cuddle in closer, close my eyes and fall asleep.

CHAPTER SIXTEEN
Rachel

I wake to light shining through the small window on the other side of the room. Sammy isn't in bed and I'm left alone with my thoughts.

Even though I don't want it to, my mind takes me back to yesterday. To my attack. I think of things that I should have done but was too scared at the time. Then I make plans in case I'm ever attacked again.

I feel like I should feel scared or helpless, but the only emotion running through my mind is anger. How dare they break into my home. How dare they rape me.

As strange as it sounds, I didn't have any nightmares. I fell asleep last night knowing, without a single doubt, that Sammy and the guys will find those three. *Antonio, Frankie, and Roman.*

I push yesterday to the back of my head, sit up, and look around the room. It isn't much. A small room with gray walls, one window, a white dresser, and this bed. But it's comfortable.

I smile when I see my chair beside the bed. I reach out and adjust it so that I can slide over.

The simple gesture of making sure my only form of mobility was right next to me makes my heart swell with love. I always feared that my legs would be the reason I stayed single for the rest of my life.

Maybe Sammy was telling the truth after all and it truly doesn't bother him.

Once I'm in my chair I make my way out of the room. The hallway is long, going in both directions, and I can see multiple doors leading to what I assume are other bedrooms.

It's like a motel but homier.

I make my way down the hall and stop at the top of the stairs.

Now, I'm a pro in this chair, but I'm not that good.

"Hello," I shout. "Crippled woman stuck at the top of the stairs."

I wait a few seconds to see if anyone responds. When no one does, I try again.

"HELLO! I REALLY HAVE TO PEE!"

"Would you like some assistance, Miss Rachel?"

I look behind me at my new favorite biker.

"Wolf," I smile. "It turns out that stairs don't always turn into escalators," I tease. "Would you mind helping me to a bathroom before I have an accident?"

Wolf smiles and his teeth are a bright contrast against his black beard and hair. He truly is a magnificent looking male.

"Of course, Miss Rachel," he says, always so polite. "There's a restroom just at the other end of this hall. It's the very last door."

"Thank you so much," I say. I turn and dash to the bathroom. My bladder sucks and I know that I don't have much time left.

Once in the bathroom, I maneuver myself onto the toilet and do my business before scooting back into my chair. I wash my hands and curse that the mirror is so far up. I wonder what I look like this morning.

I'm still wearing Sammy's shirt, my hair feels wild, and I don't think I've shaved my legs in months.

I panic for a moment before remembering that I don't really care what people think of me. If they don't like the way I look they can look somewhere else.

As for Sammy, if he truly wants to be with me then he's going to have to learn that I enjoy looking like a bum most days.

I open the bathroom door to find Wolf leaning against the wall.

"We brought over a few bags of your clothes," he informs me. "They're in Ink's room."

I thank him and make my way back to the room. If I'm getting help going down the stairs, I really want to at least be wearing panties.

I find three large black trash bags full of my clothes on the other side of the dresser. To say I'm thankful is an understatement. I manage to find a simple outfit, leggings, a long-sleeved shirt that says, Not Adulting Today, and some sandals.

Nothing to write home about but at least my butt's covered.

"I think I'm going to have to carry you down the stairs," Wolf says when I open the door. "Then I'll come back up and get your chair."

I nod and we make our way to do just that. Wolf brings me down the stairs and sits me on a small table next to the front door before retrieving my chair.

"Thank you, Wolf," I say once I'm situated back in my seat. "Just so you know, you're my favorite biker, now."

He smiles and we make our way down the hall towards voices.

I enter the room and freeze with what I see. No wonder

Sammy couldn't help me. He's got two women rubbing their half-exposed tits all over him.

Wolf clears his throat and Sammy looks our way. I turn to leave but not before I saw his face fall.

He's changed, my ass. I told myself a thousand times not to trust him.

"Baby," he shouts behind me. "Stop! It isn't what you think."

I stop and take a deep breath in.

I'm a grown-ass adult, I remind myself. I turn around and wait for him to explain.

"Those women are club Bunnies," he says, kneeling down in front of me. "They came here to give Bear the reports on some of the businesses we run. I told them that I'm not interested. They were only there less than a second before you came in the room."

I don't say anything as I watch the desperation on his face. He seems sincere and I do believe him. But that doesn't stop those damn teenage memories from surfacing.

"Alright," I finally say. "Your sexual reputation is both entertaining and annoying."

"What it was is a mistake," he says. "Never in my life have I wished I was a virgin until you came back into my life."

"Well, I wouldn't go that far," I smile. "I need you on your a-game when we have sex. I wouldn't want you licking the wrong spots, now would I?"

I laugh at his wide-eyed look and move around him to head back down the hall. Right before I get to the room, I'm stopped and twirled around. Not an easy thing to do to this chair as fast as he did. I'm impressed.

"Just so you know," he says, leaning so close that our

breaths mingle. "There is no wrong spot. I plan to lick every single inch of your body."

He walks away with a devil's smirk.

Well, he sure told me.

"ARE YOU SERIOUS?"

I'm brought out of my daze by Slim screaming. I turn to see what's going on and watch as he and Rose hug fiercely.

"I'm not happy about it, but we've agreed that if you two are ready, we are too."

Bear's facial expression doesn't match his words or his tone. Whatever it is that they're talking about, he's clearly not very happy about it.

I turn and follow Sammy to a table with Wolf, Laura, Thea, and Trigger.

"Biscuits and gravy for breakfast today," Laura says. "The kids love it."

I look at the table beside us and smile as I watch the older kids stuff their cute little faces with biscuits and gravy.

I can't wait to have children. I want a house full of beautiful little boys and girls. I want there to never be silence. I know it's a silly thing to want, but I can't wait for it.

I wonder how Sammy will react when I tell him?

I glance over only to catch him watching me with a small smile. I smile back and wait as Wolf moves a chair from the table. I scoot against the table and lock my wheels.

"By the way," I say to Sammy. "Wolf's my favorite biker. Just so you know."

I smile at Sammy as he glares at Wolf. Wolf throws his head back and laughs causing the rest of us, including

Sammy, to do the same.

"You're in trouble," Sammy informs me. "I will be your only favorite biker."

"Well, Wolf helped me pee this morning, and he carried me down the stairs while you were getting squished by four giant tits."

This time, his glare aims right for me and I laugh.

Yesterday was the worst day of my life. Even worse than when I was in the accident that lost me my legs. But, sitting here now, with a table full of laughter, a room full of family, I feel happier than I have in a long time.

And it's all because of Sammy.

CHAPTER SEVENTEEN
Ink

Rachel is minutes away from being locked in our room.

"I don't care what you say, Sammy," she says for the third time. "I don't get to see her that often and she's only here for a day."

"Then tell her to meet you here," I say. Again.

"Have you met my sister?" she says. "She is the *exact* same way she was all those years ago."

"An uptight snob who thinks she's better than everyone else?" I ask bitterly.

"EXACTLY," Rachel shouts.

I want to be angry, but her response makes me smile. Never one to keep her thoughts to herself no matter who it was about.

We're sitting in the lounge along with everyone else. They're all pretending like they aren't paying attention to our little disagreement, but I can see their heads tilt a little when we lower our voices below a scream.

Except for Trigger. He's just staring right at us. I don't even think he's blinking.

Nosey fucks.

"Then I'm coming with you," I say sternly.

"Becky hates you," she reminds me.

Becky has hated me since high school. As much as I hate to admit it, she had a good reason. I have always been attracted to Rachel. When we were seniors in high school, I asked her to go out with me and she said yes.

Of course, my stupid ass had to act all tough and mighty in front of my friends and I ended up pushing her away. Something I'll never forgive myself for.

But, before I broke my beautiful woman's heart, I was full of puppy love. Becky warned me multiple times that if I hurt her sister then she would hurt me.

I laughed it off at the time, but she didn't lie. When Rachel graduated from high school and moved away, Becky paid me a visit one evening and broke my nose.

"Her feelings about me don't matter," I tell Rachel. "All I care about is your safety. She can break my nose all she likes."

Rachel tries to hold it in, but she bursts out laughing. I see that she's been informed of her sister's little visit.

"There's no way she's ever going to be okay with us as a couple," she says once she calms down. "When I told her over the phone, I wasn't able to get another word in. I think she might be learning the witchcraft way of life at this very moment just so she can curse you."

She sits there and smiles at me.

I can't help myself. I stand and take the few steps separating us.

"I'm coming with you," I say, leaning down and placing a small kiss on her lips. "I love you, baby. It would kill me if something else happened to you."

Yeah, I'm a dick for using her attack to get my way, but it's the truth. I would simply lose my fucking mind if someone so much as looked at her wrong.

I pull back and watch as Rachel sits frozen with her

eyes closed and her lips slightly parted. She is so fucking beautiful.

"How do I say no to that?" she asks softly.

"It's simple," I say. "You don't.

I sit back down satisfied that I got my way.

◆ ◆ ◆

"You really don't have to come inside," Rachel says, as I park the car into the mom-and-pop restaurant.

So, maybe I've been complaining the whole trip over here, but it's only because I didn't want her outside of the clubhouse.

"I'm coming in," I say.

"You know that Becky is going to give you a hard time."

I know she is. I'm ready for it.

I get out and grab Rachel's chair from the trunk.

"I've been thinking of getting you a sticker for the back of this thing," I tell her when I open the door.

"Oh yeah?" she smiles. "What, may I ask, will this sticker look like?"

I wait until she's in her chair and situated before continuing.

"I was thinking one large enough to cover the entire back part of your seat," I say. "Maybe something with my face on it and 'property of Ink' written in bold letters. What do you think?"

She tosses her head back and laughs.

"That might not work for a couple of reasons," she says through her giggles.

"Why not?" I ask in mock shock.

"Well, for one, it would crinkle and ruin every time my

chair is folded."

"Fair point," I say. "What's the second reason?"

"I usually have my backpack back there, so no one would even see your sticker."

"Hmm, I'll have to rethink my plan," I say. "But I still think it's a fantastic idea."

We make our way into the restaurant to meet the demon sister.

"Be nice, Sammy," Rachel says as we head toward our waiting guest. "She's only here for today and she's heading back home. She's been on vacation and stopped by on her way back."

"How far away does she live?" I ask, hoping she says Egypt.

"About four hours."

I internally celebrate. Becky has every right to be angry with me, but that doesn't mean I want to put up with her shit on a daily basis. Even before my dumb teenage ass ruined what I had with Rachel; Becky was a bitch towards me.

"I can hear that party going on in your head," Rachel says. "Just be nice."

"I'm always nice," I mutter as we get closer to the she-devil glaring my way. "Do you think it's too late to call in a priest for an exorcism?" I ask.

Despite the glare that Rachel is now throwing my way, she laughs.

"Hey big sister," Rachel says as we reach the table. "I've missed you. How was your vacation?"

Becky smiles and leans down to hug her sister.

"It was good," she says. "It was a nice break from the constant phone calls. I'm still so sorry that I didn't answer when the hospital called."

"I told you not to worry about it," Rachel tells her. "I wasn't ready at the moment to let you know anyway."

I'm standing behind Rachel when Becky finally looks up at me. Knowing that I need to make my intentions clear, I place my hand on Rachel's shoulder.

I'm not going anywhere; I silently tell her. *No matter what you say.*

"Sam," she says curtly.

"She-devil," I respond.

And so, the night went. Constant glares from both women. Becky's glare told me that she hates my fucking guts and Rachel's glare saying, be nice.

I was nice. It's not my fault that the she-devil can't take what she dishes out.

Other than that, I sat back and let the girls enjoy their visit. I kept an eye on my surroundings and made sure that my woman had a good and safe time with her sister.

Nothing strange happened. No one approached or left any notes on the car when we left. No one was watching and everything went smoothly.

Or so I thought.

CHAPTER EIGHTEEN
Rachel

It was wonderful getting to spend some time with my sister. When she isn't spending her time in Florida with her phone off, we actually talk every single day. My sister and I are very close.

Especially since we don't really talk to our parents anymore. It's not because something drastic happened, but because we just grew apart. I know it sounds unusual, children growing apart from their parents, but we did.

So, Becky and I have always been close. I hate that we live so far apart from each other but that's the way life works sometimes. We moved to where our lives took us.

"You've been thinking pretty hard over there," Sammy says as we head back to the clubhouse.

I look over and smile at the man who takes up so much of my thoughts.

"Was just thinking about my sister," I admit. "Before you came back into my life I only ever talked to Becky and Laura. Now, there are so many people surrounding me all the time and I'm never alone."

"Does that bother you?" he asks, sounding concerned.

I think about his question. Does it bother me that I'm never alone anymore?

"Not really," I answer after almost a minute. "I actually like being around everyone there. It's been fun and a good distraction. If I was home alone then I would only lose myself in the memory over my rape."

I'm still looking at him when I answer, and I notice the subtle jerk of his chin when I mentioned my attack. I tell him every single day that it wasn't his fault. But the stubborn man won't listen to me.

"However," I continue. "There is one negative thing about all those people."

"What's that?"

"I never really get to spend any alone time with you," I say. "It's nice being around everyone, but it feels like we can't really get to know each other again with so many distractions."

It's true. Someone is always there talking to us or pulling us from a conversation we're having. I don't hate it. But I do wish that I could talk to Sammy and get to know him on a deeper level without so many people around.

It's been a little over a month since I've been staying at the Sons clubhouse and the only time we have been able to be completely alone was at night.

I also understand, probably more than most, why we can't have that alone time at the moment. I know that everyone is working hard trying to track down Roman and his cousins. I sort of know now what went on between Roman and the Infernal Sons.

I know that Roman was sent to prison for dealing drugs, sex trafficking, and kidnapping. From what I understand, the prison he was in had some sort of power failure and Roman was one of several prisoners who escaped.

I know first-hand that he's an evil man. So, staying at the biker's place until he's caught is perfectly fine by me.

Sammy pulls into the parking lot of turns off the car.

"I promise that we will get alone time as soon as I know for a fact that you will be safe outside of these walls," he says. "In fact, once this fucker is taken care of, you're going to see so much of me that you'll be sick of my perfect face."

I burst out laughing.

"You are so full of yourself," I say. "Take your perfect face and go get my chair."

Sammy smiles and salutes.

"As my lady wishes."

I smile at the memories popping into my head. Sammy and I weren't a "couple" for that long when we were in high school, but for the small amount of time that we were, he always had me laughing.

He was the type of man that would make himself look absolutely ridiculous just to make someone smile.

It doesn't appear as if that part of him has changed any.

"How many tattoos do you have?" I randomly ask when I slide into my chair.

"Many," he says, walking beside me as we make our way to the building. "I lost track."

"Do they all mean something important to you?"

Sammy opens the door for me, and I push myself inside.

"Most of them," he says. "There are a few that are just art."

I think about the tattoos of his that I've seen.

"Like the ones across your chest?" I ask.

"Been looking at my chest, have you?" he teases. "Yeah, it's art, but if you look close enough, you'll notice it's actually a phrase."

"Is it really?" I ask shocked. I've seen that tattoo multiple times over the past week, but I've never looked close enough to see that they were words. I thought it was woven vines stretching from one shoulder to the next. "What does it say?"

"Strength, respect, brotherhood, loyalty," he tells me. "It's what makes the Infernal Sons into more than a biker club. We're a family."

"Awe, that's so sweet," I say.

"Have you decided if you want ink or not?" he asks.

I shake my head.

"To be honest, I haven't even thought about it," I admit. "But that is something I want to do in the future."

"Hey guys, you're just in time for dinner," Rose says as we round the corner.

And just like that, Rachel and Sammy's time is over.

Sammy must have been looking at me and saw my face fall because he bends down and kisses me.

"Soon, baby," he whispers against my lips.

I sure do hope so. I'm not sure if I'm ready for anything sexual but I am ready for more of those sweet kisses.

I feel the ache between my legs, and I shift my hips trying to make it stop. Okay, so there may be a small chance that I might be ready for a little something sexual.

"Is there a particular reason why you're wiggling around?" Sammy asks, smirking.

I feel my face heat and quickly look away.

"ROSE, TELL EVERYONE WE'LL BE DOWN IN A BIT," he shouts.

The only response are chuckles from the other room.

"What are you doing?" I ask as he lifts me.

"I know an ache when I see one," he responds. "I want to make you feel good, baby. Nothing more."

I should tell him that I'm not ready for that. But it

would be a lie. The thought alone of Sammy between my legs makes me more wet than I have ever been.

It doesn't take long for us to make it to our room. Ink tosses me on the bed and stands above me.

"Are you okay with this?" he asks.

I nod without hesitation.

Sammy pulls at my leggings and they slide off. The coolness of the room doing nothing to calm the fire between my legs.

My panties come off next and then I'm laying here completely naked from the waist down. I can't explain why I don't feel scared. I can't explain why the men who held me down and raped me don't even enter my mind.

All I can focus on is the ache between my legs and the man who's begging to make it stop.

Ink leans down and lifts my legs up. I'm momentarily worried that he's about to find out how sex with me will be drastically different and he'll decide that I'm not worth it.

However, with a look on concentration, he leans over and grabs two pillows and piles them on top of each other. He lifts my hips and places the pillows beneath me before lowering me back down.

"There," he says. "Comfortable?"

"Strangely, yeah," I admit.

In this position, he's able to push my legs aside and out of his way.

Without another word, he leans down and attacks my most intimate area. Something he didn't even do when we were teens. I feel his tongue flicking my clit as his fingers move in and out of my hole. He doesn't pause for a single second. He feasts like a starving man.

I feel the pressure build and I grip the sheets.

Sammy is relentless as he devours my pussy. Out of nowhere, the building pressure explodes, and I scream louder than I've ever screamed.

"You taste so fucking good," he moans. "I can't seem to stop."

His licks turn gentle and he very slowly licks up and down my pussy. It's the type of lick that isn't meant to bring release, but calm one down.

"I need you, Sammy," I say, surprising us both.

"This was about you," he tells me. "Not about me."

"I need you," I repeat. "Please."

Sammy spends a few seconds looking into my eyes before he whips his pants off. His dick pops out and point right at me.

"Junior knows what he wants," Sammy chuckles.

He reaches over and grabs a condom. We haven't had the children talk yet, and I'm not sure now is the time.

"I've always been careful," he explains as he places the condom over his engorged member. "But, until I know for a fact that I'm clean, I won't allow myself the pleasure of entering you unprotected."

I want to tell him that I don't care, but he's right. And I'm thankful that he's even thinking about what's best for me when I know he's as desperate as I am for this connection.

Sammy lifts my legs and places them on his shoulders.

"You sure?" he asks as he lines his dick up with my aching hole.

"Absolutely," I say without hesitation.

Oh, so slowly, Sammy pushes himself inside of me. I feel myself stretch to fit his girth and it's the most delicious pain I've ever felt.

"So fucking perfect," he moans. "So fucking tight."

When he's in as far as he can go, he pulls back and slams back inside.

I lose it.

"Please, Sammy," I beg. "Please,"

I'm not even sure what I'm begging for, but Sammy knows.

He looks down and smirks.

"Hold on, baby," he tells me. "I'm about to brand this fucking pussy."

He didn't lie. He pistols in and out of me with relentless speed. I reach up and place my hands on the headboard to hold myself in place.

"Yes, Sammy," I moan. "I'm going to come again."

"I don't fucking think so," he tells me. "Not without me."

Sammy pushes my knees towards my chest and uses my legs for leverage as his speed increases. This new position has him deeper than ever and I close my eyes as spots cloud my vision.

His hands moves to my clit and he flicks it back and forth with the same speed of his thrusting hips.

I explode. My release the strongest I have ever felt.

"FUCK," Sammy moans. "So fucking tight."

His voice is strained and his movements jerky. A few thrusts later, he plants himself as deep inside of me as he can go and screams his own release.

"Fuck," he says, falling against me. My legs fall to either side of him as he cups my face and kisses me. I marvel at the taste of me on his tongue and suck it until all the flavor is gone.

"Fuck, baby," he moans against my lips. "I can't wait to get my cock in on that mouth action."

I laugh.

"I think they're waiting for us downstairs," I smile.

"I'm full," he says. "I've already had my meal."

We both laugh and relax in our positions. Me on my back with my hips still propped on the pillow, and Sammy over top of me licking my neck.

I could lay here forever. But we only stay for ten minutes before getting dressed and heading downstairs.

◆ ◆ ◆

We spend the evening eating dinner and playing Canasta.

"I told you it was my fucking turn," Sammy says to the table. "If you would have listened then I could have won this hand."

"You're just a sore loser," Slim grins.

"No, you're cheating somehow," Chains says to Slim.

"I am not cheating, asshole," Slim says, dropping his grin.

"Slim, you have won seven out of the nine games we've played," Brick says. "You are definitely cheating."

"Fine, you big ass babies," Slim says, shuffling the deck of cards. "Rematch."

"Let me deal," Bear grumps.

I can't help but laugh. A table full of men and they're about to go to war over a card game.

"I'm out," I say. "I'm going to go watch Frozen with the kiddos."

"Alright babe," Sammy says distractedly. "Slim, I swear, my eyes will be on you this whole time. No fucking funny business."

"Hawk, aren't you going to defend my honor?" Slim asks his man.

Hawk shakes his head.

"Nope," he says. "I'm with them. You're cheating, sweet boy."

Slim smacks the back of Hawk's head.

"Don't you sweet boy me," he says.

I shake my head and leave the competitive bunch to their battle.

Surprisingly, Rose, Bella, and Thea are no less competitive. They decide to play another round.

I make my way to Jessa and Laura.

"That was intense," I tell the girls when I stop beside the couch.

"Yeah, they usually get like that," Jessa says. "I'm actually surprised that Thea is playing because she usually doesn't play games with that bunch. They could be playing go fish and a fight would break out."

I laugh, not the least bit surprised.

"She's not kidding either," Laura adds. "I played Monopoly with them one time and swore to never again put myself through such a horrible situation."

"Mommy, I'm tired," little Bren says.

Bren is Laura's middle child and as sweet as could be.

"Yeah, it's time for bed," Laura says. "I'll be back down as soon as they're out," she tells us.

"I'm going to go put these two to bed, too," Jessa says, referring to Sophia and Daisy.

Brendon is fast asleep in a portable bassinet right beside his daddy. I've noticed that Trigger is never far from his son.

It's so sweet.

I nod my head and turn to watch the crazy group play their game. There is so much yelling and cursing that I'm not sure how Brendon is able to sleep.

I'm not sure how long I watch them play when my phone beeps from my pocket.

I smile, already knowing it's my sister. I'm surprised it took her this long.

I internally celebrate my psychic ability when I see Becky's name up on my screen.

I click on the message and see that she sent a picture. I don't have a very strong signal out here so it's taking a few minutes for the picture to load, but when it does my heart drops.

The image is of my sister tied up with blood running down the side of her face.

Her eyes are closed, and my first thought is that she's dead.

"You have five minutes to make your way outside without anyone knowing. Five minutes, Dove, or your sister dies."

Dove! That's what Roman called me. I have to stop myself from screaming for help. As scared as I feel at this moment, the thought of my sister being killed scares me even more.

I look over at the table to make sure no one is looking my way.

No one is looking.

I mentally urge someone to look.

Please, Sammy, turn around a look.

But he doesn't, He's too focused on his game.

I'm both glad and upset that he didn't look. I take a second longer to watch Sam as he concentrates on the cards in his hands.

I have a feeling that this is the last time I'm going to see him. Because I will go and save my sister, but I won't let them rape me again.

I'll kill myself first.

I turn as quietly as I can and leave the room. When I reach the front door, I take a chance and look back one more time.

Someone, please stop me.

But no one is there.

With tears clouding my vision, I open the door and make my way outside. It's storming and, at first, I can't see a thing.

"You were cutting it close, Dove."

I bite my tongue to keep from screaming as Roman Hernández steps in front of me.

"You only had twenty seconds left."

"Where's my sister?" I demand.

"Tsk, tsk. Time for us to go," he says.

In the span of a few seconds, Roman rushes forward and pulls me from my chair. I'm tossed over his shoulder and we're running.

I look up and watch as the clubhouse grows smaller and smaller. I close my eyes and picture the group of people inside full of laughter. I picture Sammy as he leans down, smiles, and kisses me so softly.

My tears are pouring down my face but are being erased by the rain as if they were never there.

It fits, really. My feelings don't matter at this moment. What matters is getting my sister away from this evil man.

Sammy will be fine. He'll eventually find Roman, but I don't think I'll be alive at that point. I can't handle being violated again. I won't let it happen.

The only liquid on my face is rain. My tears dried up with sheer determination. Somehow, I'll save my sister, and kill Roman.

Sammy and the others will be safe, my sister will be

safe, and I'll have my revenge.

Roman continues to run with me over his shoulder.

As my body jostles back and forth, the fear slowly fades away.

I smile.

Save Becky. Save Sammy. End Roman.

Even if it costs me my life, Roman's will end.

CHAPTER NINETEEN
Ink

"Come on guys, we've been on this round for over an hour now," Slim says. "I need to check my computers and get to bed."

Has it really been that long? I look at my watch and see that it's close to midnight.

"Let's call it a night," Bear says.

We all throw our cards in a pile on the table and stand. Time to get Rachel and get to bed.

I look around the empty room.

"Has anyone seen Rachel?" I ask.

"She's probably upstairs," Brick says. "Jessa, Laura, and the kids are gone, too."

Knowing he's probably right, I grab a beer from the fridge and make my way upstairs. I check our room but she's not in there. She isn't in the bathroom or any fucking room on this floor.

"INK, GET DOWN HERE RIGHT FUCKING NOW," Hawk yells.

My mind is blank as I rush down the stairs and into the office.

"We're so fucking stupid," Bear says. "Why did we let this happen? Ink is going to lose his fucking mind."

"I can't find Rachel," I say, entering the room.

"Ink, you need to watch this," Slim says.

I drag myself to the monitor and watch as Slim presses play.

I watch with dread as Rachel pulls out her phone. She has a small smile on her face as she looks up from her screen to where I was sitting.

Then the smile is replaced by fear as she looks back down. A few minutes later, she turns and leaves the room.

"Where is she going?" I ask.

Slim switches cameras and I watch as she opens the front door and leaves.

"What the fuck? She knows better than to go outside alone," I say.

Slim switches the camera view again and I watch in horror as fucking Hernández steps in front of her. They exchange a few words that we can't hear and then he tosses her over his shoulder and runs off.

I lose all strength in my body and fall to my knees.

How could I let this happen? My woman was taken by the man responsible for her rape while I was playing a fucking card game.

"Ink," Trigger says, kneeling on the floor in front of me. "We'll find her, brother. We'll find her and we'll make that mother fucker pay. But, in order to do that, you need a clear head. We need to make a plan."

"I called Ma," Bear says. "Ace is bringing over a few of the Dragon's to watch the club while we hunt."

I tune out what everyone else says and I focus on the anger in my body.

I will find my woman. And when I do, I'm never letting her out of my sight again.

Rachel

Roman ran for about twenty minutes before he tossed me into the back of a vehicle.

"You know, Dove," he says from the front of the car. "My original plan was to take Bear's woman. She is what was promised to me after all. But our last meeting made me realize that I like you better."

Rose told me all about how her father sold her to the Hernández family. I'm not sure why, we never went into detail. But, apparently, Roman was going to marry her. I'm beyond happy that she was able to escape from her old life.

"However," Roman continues when I don't respond. "I did like you better when you were feisty. Now, you're nothing but a little mouse. What's wrong, Dove?"

Is he kidding? What's wrong?

"I did what you asked," I say instead of answering his question. "Now, let my sister go."

"Don't worry, Dove," he laughs. "I keep my word. I've already sent the message to let her go. Unharmed."

"How do I know you're telling me the truth?" I ask.

"You'll just have to take my word for it."

Taking his word for it isn't something I want to do but it's clear that it's the only hope I have.

I don't say anything else and just hope that he's being honest.

"I can prove it," he says five minutes later. "She really is just fine."

I'm surprised at how much he wants me to believe him.

"Prove it," I challenge.

"Call her," he says, tossing my cell in the seat beside me.

To say I'm surprised would be an understatement. I press one and hit dial.

"Rachel, why the hell did you do it?"

Hearing Becky's voice sends tears down my face.

"Becky, are you okay?" I ask.

"I'm fine," she says, clearly angry. "They told me they were going to use me to get to you. Why didn't you stay with Sam?"

"Listen," I say, not caring if Roman hears. "I need you to call Sammy and tell him that I'm fine. Tell him that I love him. I always have and I always will."

"Damnit, Rachel. I'm already on my way over there. Don't do anything stupid. Sam won't stop until he finds you."

"That's enough," Roman says.

A second later the call drops.

"How did you do that?" I demand, furious that I can't kick the back of his seat like a child throwing a tantrum.

"Cell phone blocker," he says simply. "I was starting to get a little jealous. Now you know I was telling you the truth and your sister is just fine."

"Fine," I say. "Now tell me where you're taking me and what you have planned."

"I'm taking you home," he answers. "And to be quite honest, I have no idea of our future plans. Only that we will be together."

"Over my dead body."

"There she is," he laughs. "My feisty, soon to be, bride. My father is expecting us. You see, he's forgiven me and has accepted me back into the family. All, I had to do was kill one of the Sons. And I did just that."

"I will never be your bride," I declare. "And I don't know who you killed, but it wasn't a Son."

"Yeah, well my father doesn't need to know that. Just keep your delicious mouth shut and we'll both make it through this meeting alive."

Well, thank you for the tip. I have absolutely no intention of marrying this man. I have no intention of keeping my mouth shut. If Roman is afraid of his father, then that's something I can use to my advantage.

I close my eyes and pray for the first time in years. I've never been a religious person, but I know for a fact that tonight is my last night alive and I don't want to spend eternity down below.

I can only hope that I'm not too late in that regard.

CHAPTER TWENTY
Ink

"I am getting extremely tired of our people getting taken and hurt," Bear says. "This is the last time this shit happens."

I nod my head in agreement and go back to following Hernández's tracks.

"These tracks are too obvious," Wolf says. "He's not at all afraid of being caught."

"Maybe he was counting on the storm to wash any trace of him away," Hawk says. "It would have worked if it hadn't stopped raining."

"His footprints stop here," Wolf says, pointing at the highway.

"That's why he wasn't trying to hide his trail," Bear says. "He knew that once he was in a vehicle there would be no way for us to follow him."

"FUCK!"

I take a deep breath and try to calm my racing heart. Hernández didn't even take Rachel's chair. She won't be able to escape him. She will have no choice but to stay and do as she's told.

"Hey, wait up," Slim yells, running towards us.

"Has anyone ever considered checking Hernández's father's place?" Slim pants.

"Always the reasonable and clear-headed one," I say.

"Not really, Rachel's sister Becky just showed up," Slim admits. "She told me that she was taken by Hernández in order to lure Rachel in. She was released not long ago and headed straight here. She told me that they had her at some mansion."

Without another word, we all turn and head for our bikes.

Please, be there, baby.

Rachel

While my addled brain storms through ideas on how to kill Roman, we pull up to a beautiful house. Well, it looks more like a mansion.

"Welcome to the Hernández estate," Roman says proudly. "My father raised me in this house. I plan to raise our children here as well."

I say nothing when all I want to do is freaking scream.

"My father is inside waiting, Dove, let's go."

He exits the car and starts walking towards the house.

Run my brain shouts. I guess it forgot that my legs are useless.

Roman turns around and I see that he's laughing.

"I actually forgot that you can't walk," he says when he opens the back door.

He leans into the car and I do the only thing I can. I poke him in the eye. And I'm not gentle about it.

"Damnit, woman," he shouts. "Leave that feisty attitude for when we're in our room."

"Don't mind your cousins sloppy seconds, I see," I mock.

I'm satisfied when I see how red and puffy his right eye is.

"Yeah, that was probably a mistake on my part," he says, reaching into the car again. "Put the finger away, woman."

My hands are in my lap as he picks me up like his actual bride. I don't want to fight him every time because I need him surprised when the time is right.

"You know," I say. "You're really not all that attractive."

I hear someone laugh as Roman frowns.

"He gets his looks from his Madre," a man says.

I turn my head and see an older version of Roman standing in front of us.

"I don't know," I say, apparently asking for death. "He's the spitting image of you. You must be his father."

The man laughs.

"You were right, mijo," the man says. "She is feisty."

"Papa," Roman says, smiling. "This is my new bride, Rachel. Dove, this is my father."

"I would say nice to meet you," I say. "But, in reality, I hope you both drop dead."

The man laughs again. There's something wrong with this family.

"Did she do that to your eye, mijo?"

"Si, Papa," Roman smiles. "It's a good thing her legs don't work, or she'd have probably escaped already."

They both laugh as we head towards the beautiful house.

It took almost an hour to get here from where Roman tossed me in the car. Sammy's probably noticed by now that I'm gone. I know he'll be angry when he finds out that I left willingly.

I can only hope that my sister makes it there quickly to let him know that I love him and that I'm fine.

I know Becky was right when she said that Sammy won't stop looking. I just hope that when he does eventually find my body, he'll find Roman's and his father's there with me.

I think back to the fear on Rose's face when she told me about this family. I think back to the looks of sadness on multiple faces when I was told of their friend, Princess, and how she was murdered by this family.

I think of all the women that these men have sold as sex slaves. Of all the families ruined because of the drugs that they sell on the streets.

"You are going to make a beautiful queen to our empire, Mija," Roman's father says, closing the door behind us as we enter the house.

I look around and am floored by the beauty within. There is a fantastic glass chandelier hanging above, marble flooring, and a double grand staircase to the floor above.

"I see being a criminal can lead to a life of luxury," I say.

"Only if you're good at it," Roman says. "The Hernández Cartel is known far and wide. You will never do without or be alone."

While the words themselves are meant as a comfort, the tone is anything but. It's a warning.

"Of course, I won't be alone," I mutter. "I'll be surrounded by all of the buried bodies of your victims."

"She's not wrong," his father says.

I can feel my eyes trying to mist over, but I won't show any signs of weakness in front of these men. They already think I'm weak and incapable of escaping because of my inability to walk.

While they might be right about not being able to escape, I'm anything but weak. You don't go through the crap that I have in my life and come out weak.

I just need to be patient and keep my head clear. I need the perfect plan.

As we head into the most beautiful living room that I have ever seen, an idea starts to form.

"You made sure when you killed the biker that no one else saw, right?" his father asks.

Roman tightens his hold on me before talking. A warning to keep my mouth shut.

"Of course, papa. No one was around. His body won't be found for weeks."

Roman's father doesn't say anything else. I'm finally put down on a leather couch near a beautiful fireplace.

"Can I get you anything, Mija?" his father asks. I really need to learn the man's name.

"Something sharp and shiny," I answer with more bravado than I feel.

"Your bride has balls of steel, mijo," he laughs. "I don't think you should sleep in the same bed as her."

"Not to worry, papa," Roman says. "Her hands will be secured."

Okay, starting to freak out.

"Uncle, Carlos," a new voice says. "Mi papa is on video waiting for you and Roman to join."

Carlos. I finally have a name.

"Let's go, mijo," Carlos says. "My brother doesn't like to be kept waiting."

I start to shiver. Seeing as how it isn't all that cold in here, it has to be from the adrenaline leaving my body.

"Would you like me to sit you by the fire?" Roman asks. I nod my head.

I'm lifted and placed on the soft rug in front of the fire.

"Don't try anything stupid," he warns. "I can see you

from the office."

As Roman walks off, I stare into the fire and formulate my plan.

Step number one is to act more vulnerable than I actually am.

My face starts overheating so I search for the iron tools to helps extinguish the fire only to find a knob instead.

It's gas. I turn the knob down until the fire is barely there.

"What are you doing?" Roman asks from behind me.

"I got hot," I answer. "I wasn't able to move away so I turned down the fire. I hope that was okay."

I've never been a good liar. I am fully capable of moving completely across this room if I wanted. I hope my face looks as vulnerable as I want him to think I am.

"Of course, Mija," Carlos says, coming into the room. "He shouldn't have put you so close."

"Time to get some rest, love," Roman says, lifting me up. "Tomorrow we marry."

The knot in my stomach tightens even further.

"Look," I say. "I came to you of my own free will. I don't want the Sons or my sister hurt so I'll do whatever you want. But I ask that you please not tie me up. Heck, I would be content to just watch that fire all night long. It's not like I can run away."

Roman smiles. "Lucky for you, we have a fireplace in our room."

"I will be locking your door from the outside, mijo," Carlos says. "I'm sure you can handle her inside the room by yourself. If you need me to unlock your door, just call my room."

Roman nods and walks up the stairs.

So, Carlo's is locking us both into the room.

Roman reaches what I assume is his room and walks inside. It's dark outside and the lights in the room are off, so I can't see much of anything. Carlos reaches in and flips a switch causing a smaller chandelier to illuminate the room.

"See you in the morning, Mija," Carlo's smiles. "Tomorrow, you will become family."

He shuts the door and I hear the lock click in place.

"I'm tired, Dove," Roman says. "Time for bed."

Panic rushes through my body.

"Remember," he continues. "Killing me won't do you any favors. My father would make your life painful if you did so. It's not fun being used as a sex toy for anyone who pays."

I let the tears finally fall. I'm so freaking scared.

Roman laughs.

"Yeah, she gets it," he says to himself.

He lays me down on one side of the bed and covers me up before starting the fire and turning off the lights.

"Goodnight, Dove," he says, laying down on the other side of the mattress.

The bed is so large that two more people could lay down between us and we would still have room to sleep comfortably.

No complaints from me.

It doesn't take long for Roman to fall asleep. I don't know how long I lay there watching the flames and listening to the man breathe, but I know that it was a very long time. When I know for a fact that he is asleep as deep as he could be, I quietly sit up.

Getting to the floor without making a sound is going to be hard. Especially considering how far up this bed is. Luckily, he's so far away that he won't feel any small movements I make.

Taking a chance, I dive hands first to the floor. With some maneuvering, I manage to get my whole body on the floor with next to no noise.

I'm brought back to the memory of my first visit with Roman where I had to do this exact same thing.

Fate's funny.

I check to make sure Roman is still asleep before I scoot towards the fireplace. I'm exhausted and I need to desperately take a deep breath, but I fear that my panting will wake him.

So, I'm taking small shallow breaths. My chest is burning from lack of oxygen, my arms are weak from pulling the weight of my whole body and my heart feels like it's about to beat out of my chest.

But I make it.

Not wanting to waste even a second of time, I reach for the controller and turn until the fire is completely out.

But not the gas.

I remember a blog I read online a couple of years back about a family who fell asleep safely tucked in their beds only to be found dead by a family member the next day.

A gas leak, it said. They all went peacefully in their sleep.

With the door shut, it shouldn't take more than an hour for the gas to take effect in this room.

Roman dying in his bed while he sleeps isn't how I've been envisioning his death. But I'll take it.

I lay down in front of the fireplace and close my eyes. It doesn't take long before I start to feel lightheaded. Just as I feel myself drift off an evil chuckle reverberates through my head.

"Nice try, Mija," the chuckling man says. "That idiot

son wasn't able to see through to your plan, but it was as clear as day to me. Plans have changed. We will let my son sleep until death and you will join me in my room."

I'm trying everything to stay awake, but I just can't. I feel myself being lifted. I see myself screaming, biting, and hitting, but nothing more than a whimper escapes my lips.

Right before I succumb to darkness, I watch as Carlos locks Roman's door, leaving his own son to die.

CHAPTER TWENTY-ONE
Ink

"What do you mean he's fucking dead?" We arrived with the Hernández estate in turmoil. It was surrounded by police cars and paramedics.

"There was a gas leak and everyone inside is dead," Bear says. "According to one of the officers, there were seven people total."

I stop breathing as I wait for him to continue.

"She's not inside," he says. "There were no females present at all. They found Hernández and the security staff."

I collapse against my bike in both relief and fear.

"Then where the fuck is my woman?" I ask.

"Excuse me, can I ask you all a few questions?"

The last thing I want is to be stuck here for hours answering questions.

"I can handle this," Bear says. "You all head back and I'll meet you there."

I straddle my bike and wait to hear what the officer has to say.

"You're positive Roman Hernández is in that building?" Bear asks.

"Yes," the officer says. "He fell asleep and was killed because of a gas leak."

"There's something he isn't telling us," Wolf says.

I'm startled because I thought he left. I look back and see that, in fact, no one has left. They're all listening.

"What are you hiding?" Bear asks.

"I'm not at liberty to say," the officer responds.

"Oh, lighten up probie. Give the Sons what they want."

"Hey, it's Detective Dick. I mean Rick Anderson," Brick says.

Surprisingly, the detective laughs.

"Not the first time I've been called that, and I know it won't be the last," he says, shaking Bear's hand.

"Last time I saw you I was putting handcuffs on Roman and his father. Not that I'm surprised, but why are you all out here?"

I watch Bear to follow his signal. As our Prez, it's up to him on how much information we give.

I want nothing more than to barge through every man here and search for my woman, but without something more to go on, there's nowhere for me to go. So, I wait.

"One of our own was taken," Bear says. "A woman. We have reason to believe that it was Roman."

"What reasons?" Detective Rick asks.

"I'd rather not say," Bear answers.

The detective doesn't say anything for a few seconds as he thinks through what Bear said.

"There are no women inside this house," Rick says. "Roman is inside along with several of his security goons."

"What about his father?" I ask. "Is he inside?"

Rick shakes his head. "There is no sign of Carlos Hernández," Rick says. "Every gas line was wide open when we arrived, and Roman's bedroom door was locked from the outside. We have reason to believe that this was no accident."

"He has her," Trigger declares. "The head of the fucking Hernández Cartel has our woman."

"Anything I should know," Rick asks.

"Just know that if you find Carlos before us that he most likely has one of our women. Remember that before you go in guns blazing," Bear says.

"Brother's, let's go."

"Wait," I say. "Why are you here anyway?"

"We've had someone on the place since the Hernández's escaped," Rick answers. "He missed his check-in an hour ago. We found him near his car with his throat slit."

"Ink, shut the fuck up, and let's go."

I nod at Rick before flipping off Chains.

Without a second more wasted, we all start our bikes and follow Bear back to the clubhouse. It's time for Slim to do his thing.

Rachel

"What if I told you that you could rule my empire alongside me?" Carlos asks.

I'm sitting in the front passenger seat of some fancy looking vehicle. The seats feel leather and everything just looks futuristic.

I hate it.

"Well," I say calmly. "I would definitely want to change a few things."

"Oh, yeah?" he says, completely interested in what I have to say.

"Mm-hm."

"Like what?" he asks.

"Well, I would spend the rest of my life destroying you from the inside," I admit. "Every breath I take would be for the sole purpose of your destruction. However, if I could pull it off, I would kill you early on. Then dismantle your empire brick by brick until the only thing left would be the dirt you once stood on."

I look over at Carlos and smile at the shock on his face.

"Unexpected," he eventually says. "I'll give you a few weeks to rethink your answer. I think some time with my girls will do the trick."

Sex slaves. I know that's what he's talking about. The fear in my soul tries to take over as I'm thrown back to the day I was attacked.

I close my eyes and picture Sammy. His image is all I need to find my strength.

"Why is my answer unexpected?" I ask, opening my eyes. "Did you really think I would roll over like a dog and beg you for attention? The very sight of you makes me sick.

You can try all you like, but nothing you say or do

will break me down. I'm a survivor. Rape me, beat me, or break my body. The only difference you will see is the physical."

"That's big talk for someone who can be beaten or killed at any moment," he says, jaw tight.

He's mad. Good.

"You really think that bothers me?" I ask. "The fact that you might kill me at any moment is what I'm most hopeful for. You killed your own son. I would expect nothing less from a man with no soul."

"I have a soul," he laughs. "It's just owned by the devil."

What do I say to that?

"We're here," he says, parking the car in front of an old run-down trailer.

"Where's here, exactly?" I ask. I don't know what my future holds but I plan to gather every bit of information along the way.

"Your home for the next couple of weeks," he answers. "You remember Antonio and Frankie, right? Roman told me all about your meeting."

"My meeting?" I ask, angry. "They raped me."

"They were just having a little fun," he chuckles.

I watch as the two men exit the trailer and head right towards us. My heart beats faster with every step closer. I want to beg for Carlos to start the car and drive away. But, rationally, I know that being with Carlos is no safer than being stuck with these two.

"You will obey them," Carlos tells me. "You will be a good girl and do what you're told, or I can make life so much worse for you."

"Whatever you say," I bravely reply. All bravado I thought I had earlier flew out the window the second one of the men opened the door. It's the man who held me down.

"Well, hey there little slut, you ready to spend some time with us?"

"Antonio, take the girl inside and show her to her room."

So, the man who held me down is Antonio. Which means the one who raped me is Frankie.

"Sure thing, tío," Antonio says. "So, you still can't walk, huh?"

"Of course, I can walk, you idiot," I lie. "I just choose not to."

Antonio stares at me with wide eyes and a slack jaw.

Moron.

"She's teasing," Carlos chuckles. "You must carry her, Sobrino."

"No puedo esperar a mi turno. Mi polla le enseñará modales a esta puta."

Crap. Now he's speaking Spanish. I really should have paid closer attention in high school Spanish class.

"It's not nice to call women, whores, Antonio," Carlos says. "Take her inside. And keep your dick in your pants."

"Esto es una mierda," he says, lifting me roughly and tossing me over his shoulder.

"Bullshit or not, do as I fucking say."

Carlos may be an evil man, but I appreciate his last order. Not that it would stop these men if they really wanted to rape me again.

I won't let it come to that.

"I'll be back in a few hours," Carlos says from beside the car. "If I find out that either of you has laid a single finger on her when I get back, I'll fucking kill you."

It's extremely dark outside, so all I see as he drives away are the red taillights.

"I'm not worried," Frankie says. "He wouldn't kill us, we're family."

I'm tossed onto a hard couch, hitting my head on the wooden armrest.

"I wouldn't be so sure about that," I say, wincing when I feel the new bump rising up on my head. "He killed Roman right before tossing me in his car and driving here."

I look around the room. The walls are covered in a yellowed flower wallpaper, the carpet is stained a dark brown and everything is filthy. There's trash all over the coffee table and the floor.

"She's lying, Antonio," Frankie finally says. "Carlos wouldn't kill his own son."

"Why would I lie?" I ask. "Obviously your uncle doesn't hold family at a level you thought he did."

I scoot my body until I'm against the back of the couch. The room is starting to blur, and it feels like I could pass out at any second.

"Damnit, Tonio, how hard did you throw her on the couch?"

I miss whatever it is they say next because the room goes black and I fade away into a less frightening world.

CHAPTER TWENTY-TWO
Ink

The sun came up a few hours ago and we are no closer to finding Rachel. I know that Slim is working tirelessly trying to find even the smallest bit of information, but I can't help but feel fucking pissed.

"Bud, I need you to relax or go take a walk," Slim tells me, not taking his attention from his screens.

"I'm not going to take a fucking walk, Slim," I growl.

Hawk gives me a warning look. It isn't the first time I've taken my anger out on Slim and it appears my brother is about had it.

"One more time, brother," Hawk tells me calmly. "I understand that you're scared and stressed but if you talk to my man with anything other than respect one more time then you and I are going to have problems."

I close my eyes and take a deep breath.

"I'm sorry, Slim," I say. I walk over and rest my forehead on top of Slim's head. "Please, don't be mad at me."

"Think nothing of it, Ink," he says, reaching up and petting my hair. "I do understand. But your constant pacing is a huge distraction. I can't be panicked or distracted while I'm searching this deep, I might miss something."

He's right, of course. I straighten and walk to Hawk.

"We're going to find her, brother," he says, grabbing my

arm and pulling my head to his. Much like he and Bear do. Their twin bond is the strongest I've ever seen between siblings.

"We're going to find her," he repeats. "And, this time, we won't make the mistake of leaving a single Hernández alive."

"Ink, can I get a hand?"

I accept more of Hawk's strength before walking towards Bella.

"Sure thing, pretty lady," I say. "What can I do?"

Bella takes me over to where Sophia is crying in her highchair

"She won't stop crying," Bella tells me over the wailing of her daughter. "I think she can feel everyone's anxiety. Do you think you could give it a shot?"

I smile.

"Absolutely," I say, leaning over to pick up Sophia. "What do you say we go have a seat on the couch?"

I hand Sophia to Trigger before running upstairs to get my guitar. I haven't played my guitar since Rachel came back into my life. I used to use it as a way to pick up chicks. I won't tell my woman that when I play for her one day.

"How about a song?" I ask, sitting on the coffee table in front of Trigger and Sophia. "This one always makes the girls smile."

I strum the chords and start singing.

It doesn't take but a few seconds for little Sophia to stop crying.

By the time I make it through that song, I'm ready to play another. After about the fifth song, Sophia is fast asleep in Trigger's arms and I am feeling much more relaxed.

I nod to Trigger and make my way back into the office.

"There's no way for us to even get close enough to look," Hawk says as I walk into the room. "It would be next to impossible to get in without getting caught. That place is a fortress. It's more secure than the White House."

"Maybe not," Slim says. "I have an idea, but Ink might not like it."

"Worst idea ever," I say, smiling. "So, what's this idea that I hate?"

Slim, Hawk and Bear all turn to look at me.

"We want to make sure the entire Hernández Cartel gets taken down for good," Slim says.

"I don't hate that idea at all," I assured him. "In fact, I am all for it."

"Yeah, that's not all," Slim says, looking guilty.

"We need to find a way inside of their home base," Bear tells me.

I shake my head. "Like Hawk said, it's completely fortified. That's why we haven't even attempted it yet."

"That was before we had someone on the inside," Slim says. "Before you get angry, hear me out. We know that Carlos Hernández killed his son, took Rachel, and left. Seeing as how the estate is now in police custody, that leaves only one place left. He's going to take her to a place where he knows we can't get to her."

I shake my head, already knowing where Slim is heading.

"If I can find a way to contact Rachel while she's there," Slim rushes to say before I have a chance to speak. "Then she might be able to help us infiltrate the compound without getting caught. We can save her and take down the entire Cartel at once."

"Not fucking happening," I avowed. "No way are we risking her life more than it already is."

"Besides," Wolf says, coming to stand beside me. "That plan all hinges on her being taken by Carlos. There's always a possibility that she wasn't."

"Even if she was," Trigger adds, leaning against the door. "She isn't going to have free range of anything. She would be a prisoner and most likely locked up."

"Those are all valid points," Slim admits. "But the fact remains that this is our only option. I'm sorry to be so blunt here, Ink, but if Rachel is inside that compound, then there is no way in hell we are going to be able to rescue her without inside help. She's the only choice we have to both save her and take down that horrible family."

He's right. I hate to admit it, but he's right.

"Alright," I say, flopping down in Bear's chair. "You were right. I hate this plan. But it really is our only option. That is assuming that Carlos has Rachel and that he took her to that damn compound."

Slim turns back to his computer screens. "I've been hacking into a few different systems that are associated with the compound. I have access to any appointments made with their lawyer, doctor, hitman, grocery delivery service. You name it, I'm safely hidden inside their systems. All I have to do is monitor and look for our best chance."

Slim turns back around and looks me in the eyes.

"I'm not going to lie to you, Ink," he tells me. "This could take a very long time. I'm talking weeks or even months. We have to be careful. Any wrong move will alert someone to what I'm doing and our only chance at contacting Rachel will be gone."

Months? My beautiful woman could be a captive for months? There's no telling what they will do to her in that time. The thought alone makes me sick.

"I'll have someone watching the compound at a safe distance every single day and night, brother," Bear says. "We will always have eyes on the entrance. If for some reason, she leaves the compound we will take that opportunity and grab her."

"Bear's right," Chains adds, walking into the room with a handful of beers. "If we come upon a situation where we can get her back with a simple grab, then we'll do it. Fuck the compound. Family comes first, revenge second."

"Until then," Bear continues. "We'll stick with Slim's plan. I think it's safe to remove the lockdown. Roman Hernandez was the one targeting our family and now he's dead. Tell everyone to go home, but not to let their guards down."

I accept the beer Chains holds out.

"Why don't you stay with us?" Chains says. "My house is closer to the clubhouse than yours and we could keep each other company."

I know what he really means. He wants to keep an eye on me to make sure my head stays on straight. I appreciate it, but it's really unnecessary.

"Thanks, man," I say. "But I think I'll either be here or over at the shop."

"Alright, brother. The offer stands in case you change your mind."

I take my beer and head upstairs to my room. The first thing I see when I open the door is Rachel's chair sitting on her side of the bed. Wolf most likely brought it up here. I flop down on the bed and try to get some shut eye.

But sleep never comes. Every time I close my eyes all I

see is Rachel being beaten or raped.

I can't just sit around here doing nothing. I'm telling Bear that I'm going to be one of the eyes on the Hernández compound. That way I'm right there ready to move in the very first chance we get.

Even if it takes months.

CHAPTER TWENTY-THREE
Rachel

Carlos comes waltzing through the trailer door a few hours later.

The first thing he does is walk over and toss me a bottle of water.

"Did they touch you?" he asks me.

I can't wrap my head around why he sounds so concerned. He threatened me in the car. He told me that I was going to be used as a sex slave. Now, he's all concerned if I've been touched or not?

"No," I answer, opening the water and drinking.

Drugged or not, my lips are cracked, and my throat is dry. I need to drink the water.

"Good."

"Is it true, tío?" Frankie asks. "Did you really kill Roman?"

Carlos looks at me with raised brows.

"Oops," I shrug, causing him to laugh.

What a strange man.

"Roman stopped being my son the second he let the Infernal Sons rescue the woman I chose to be his," Carlos says. "Not to mention he tried to fool me into thinking he actually killed an Infernal Son. He got what he rightly deserved."

Frankie and Antonio stare at their uncle with shocked

expressions.

"The biker gang can't seem to let go of things," Carlos continues. "Which is why I've decided to take *mi Reina* and bunker down at the compound. No place better to protect someone you love."

Wait, what? Did he say, love? Doesn't *Reina* mean princess? No, that isn't right.

"Queen?" I ask. "I'm not your queen and if the past day tells me anything, it's that I wouldn't want to be someone you think you love."

Carlos simply laughs.

"Fantastic, isn't she?" he asks his nephews. "Absolute perfection."

Antonio finally snaps out of his shock-induced state and walks towards me.

"I wouldn't trust her, tío," he tells Carlos. "It looks like she's planning something."

"I would be disappointed if she weren't," Carlos grins. "We'll be going now. See you later, *sobrinos*."

Carlos picks me up and carries me back to his car. He's handling me gently and I don't like it. I don't want to have any soft feelings towards this man. I know the second he decides to, I'll be thrown to the wolves.

I can't trust him, no matter how kind he's acting. He's the devil disguised as an angel and I need to never forget that.

"I've been thinking," he tells me as he's backing out of the driveway. "Your inability to submit to me might have its merits."

"Is that so?"

"Absolutely," he chuckles. "I rather enjoy the sass that comes out of your mouth."

"Where are you taking me?" I ask, ignoring his comment.

"Home, *mi Reina*," he says, calling me his queen again. "Where we can get to know one another a bit better."

My eyes roll at his words before I can stop them.

"I know all that I need to know about you, Carlos. So, if you would be so kind as to let me out right here, I would appreciate it."

"As much as I enjoy your sass," He says, voice dropping. "You would be wise to filter what comes out of those lips. I have no qualms about having you beaten."

"Of that, I have no doubt," I admit. "But you need to realize that I will never submit to you. No matter how many times you have me beaten or violated. I'm simply going to be a waste of your energy. Just kill me. I'd rather be dead than be considered your queen, anyway."

Carlos doesn't say anything more as he drives us to this compound he's talking about. It takes less than thirty minutes to arrive.

I can see why it's called a compound. It looks like a prison. The building is very large. I can't see very many windows, but I can tell that the building was probably an old factory of some sort. The property is surrounded by a tall, barbed wired fence that looks impossible to climb.

The rising sun gives the image an almost beautiful glow.

We stop in front of the gate and wait as two people push open the metal doors. The fear slams into my chest because I know that once I'm inside of this fence, I'm never leaving.

We drive through the now opened gate and when I hear the final click of the heavy doors closing, I let my tears fall.

"Now, now," Carlos says softly. "No need to cry, my

dear, as long as you obey, you are going to love your new life."

"That's the problem," I admit. "I have absolutely no intentions of obeying a single thing you say."

Carlos chuckles.

"You will, *mi Reina*. You won't have a choice in the matter."

I don't respond. It would be useless.

Carlos stops in front of the building.

"I bought a wheelchair for you," Carlos says. "I also came here to prepare the place for your arrival. That's why I was gone so long. I think you will be satisfied."

He leaves the car and walks around to my side. My first thought is to lock the door. But what good would that do? Not only does he have the keys in his hands, but I would simply be stuck inside the car until someone broke a window and forced me out.

Carlos picks me up and carries me inside the building. I look around horrified.

My first assumption was correct. This is an old prison. There are prison cells lining the walls of the hallway we're currently in.

"Until I can trust you, you will be living here," he tells me. "When you learn to submit to my authority and accept your role by my side, I will have you moved to my floor. Trust me, it's much roomier and nicer than this one."

He takes me inside the very last cell in the hallway and places me in a child sized wheelchair.

"This was the only chair available on such short notice," he tells me. "It's a bit small but it gets the job done. I've had an actual bed brought in, along with a television and some movies. There's a working toilet over in the corner. If you need help, just let someone know."

I remain silent as he backs out of my new prison and locks me inside.

"This is for your own good," he tells me. "I never wanted to resort to this, but I know that you'll give me a hard time if I let you roam around."

He's not wrong. I hated the man before but as I stare at him on the other side of the bars, I feel anger flood me like never before.

"I will ask you only one time per day if you've changed your mind. If I don't like your answer, I will have you whipped. Do you understand?"

I don't move a muscle.

"This is going to hurt me more than it will you," he says. "Mike, please come here."

A man comes to stand next to Carlos. Where Carlos is an attractive older male, with gray hair, laugh lines on his face, and life in his eyes, this new man is the complete opposite.

He's large. Towering over Carlos type of large. His face is full of scars, he's completely bald and his eyes look dead.

This man has been through a lot of life and none of it looks good. I sort of feel sorry for him.

"Mike, I would like you to use the whip and punish her with ten lashes to her back. Don't be gentle."

Carlos leaves and Mike smiles.

Never mind. Any sympathy I felt for him moments ago vanish as he opens my cell door.

He rushes forward and pulls me up. The next thing I know, I'm flat down on the bed and the back of my shirt is ripped open.

"Don't struggle," Mike warns. "Or this will be far less

pleasant."

A high-pitched whistle grabs my attention and I try to turn but stop when a burning sensation races across my back.

"I always go easy on the first strike," Mike chuckles. "Just to give you a small taste of what's to come."

That was easy? Tears fill my eyes, but I refuse to let them fall.

Mike strikes my back again and the tears fall as I hold in my scream. He can have my tears, but I refuse to give him my voice.

Strikes three, four, and five land. My back is burning so bad that it feels like it's on fire.

"Boss has himself a strong one," Mike says.

By the time strike six lands on my back, I can no longer hold back my screams.

The strikes eventually stop, and I hear the cell door open and close.

"Every day, *mi Reina*," I hear Carlos say. "Until you submit."

"I... am... not... your... queen," I pant.

"Every day," he repeats.

The lights turn off and I'm left in my prison completely alone. I use my arms to push my body up only to fall back down with the pain that shoots around my back.

It would be so easy to just give in and give him what he wants. It would be so easy to find something in this cell and end my life.

But, at this very moment, I have decided that I will do neither. I will fight Carlos every step of the way. It will eventually lead me to freedom, or it will lead me to death.

But I will NEVER be his queen.

CHAPTER TWENTY-FOUR
Ink

It's been two weeks since Rachel went missing. Two weeks of restless nights, and busy days. If I could, I would spend every single moment on lookout duty next to the Hernández compound, but my family won't leave me the fuck alone.

They demand that I eat, sleep and bathe. It pisses me off, but I'm beyond grateful for it. I need to be at full strength if there comes a day when we're ready to get her out of there.

"Carlos has only left those damn gates twice in the two weeks we've been watching," Wolf says.

"What kind of traffic do they have?" Hawk asks.

"Not much," I answer. "They have a shipment of women coming in once a week using an ice-cream truck. Apart from that, there are your basic vehicles going in and out, but it doesn't happen but a few times a day."

I'm sitting in Hawk's kitchen with all of my brothers except Chains. He's on watch until I get back to the compound later today.

I would never have left if Slim hadn't called an emergency meeting.

"Are you ever going to tell us why we're here?" Bear asks. "I was in the middle of a nap."

"You live next door, old man," Slim chuckles. "It's not like you had to drive to get here."

Despite the constant fear for Rachel that lives inside me, I laugh. Our prez isn't much older than I am, but his role as President to the Infernal Sons tends to wear him down.

"Sweet boy," Hawk says. "Be nice to my twin. He can't help it if he's grumpy. You ruined his nappy time."

Everyone laughs. Including Bear.

"Okay," Slim says. "I called you all here for a reason so let's get this meeting started."

I grab a beer from the fridge and make myself comfortable.

"As you all know, I've been spending my life monitoring any and all signals coming to and from the Hernández compound. The first thing I noticed is that they order a lot, and I mean a crap ton, of frozen pizzas."

"I don't think their food preferences are going to help us much," Hawk teases.

"I know that, big guy," Slim smiles. "I just wanted you all to know that my addiction to popcorn is nothing compared to their frozen pizza addiction."

"I'm not so sure about that," I say. "You can go through a truckload of popcorn in a week."

"And you don't share," Trigger growls.

"*Anyway,* I also noticed that there are next to no females inside the compound."

"How do you know that for sure?" Bear asks.

Slim pulls out his laptop and taps away.

"For some stupid reason, they have a roster online of every single member inside that gate."

Slim turns his computer around showing us the list of every member of the Hernández Cartel.

"There has to be hundreds of names there," I say.

"Five-hundred and seventy to be exact," Slim explains. "They're not all there at the same time, usually only up to fifty, but they're all listed. And of that five-hundred and seventy names, there is only one female. A baby named Gabby. From what I gathered, one of the men who live on the property is a single parent and they let his daughter stay there with him."

"While this information is odd, what good is it going to do for Rachel?" I ask, trying not to sound frustrated.

"Patience grasshopper," Slim jokes. "Anyway, a little over an hour ago, a doctor's appointment was booked for someone inside the compound. The person isn't listed by name, but we do know where and when they're going to be."

Slim pauses.

"While this person isn't listed by name, it is listed that it's a woman in her late twenties."

"We have our in," Bear exclaims.

"Yes," I agree. "But why the fuck does she need to see a doctor?"

"As hard as it is," Hawk says calmly. "We need to not think about that and focus on how to contact her."

"I have an idea," Wolf says. "Slim, do you have any device small enough for her to hide?"

Slim nods.

"Okay," Wolf continues. "They've never seen my face before, so I can take the small device and find a way to hand it off to Miss Rachel while she's at the Doctor's office."

"Why not just grab her then?" Slim asks.

"It could get them both killed," I explain. "Plus, as much as I hate this part, we need Rachel inside to help us find a way in and end this fucking family."

"I'll do my best to explain things to Miss Rachel when I see her," Wolf says. "If she is not on board with our plan, I will get her out of there one way or another."

I nod my head. It kills me to let another man go to her side when I know where she's going to be. But Carlos knows my face.

We sit down and make our plans. Rachel's appointment is tomorrow morning at eight. It's going to take everything I have to keep myself from barging into that building, killing every mother fucker in my way, and taking my woman back.

I'll be on standby in case Rachel tells Wolf that she wants out now. I'll be right there waiting for her, just in case.

"It's almost time, sister," Bella says quietly. "We're so close to bringing you home."

I look up and smile at the beautiful Bella holding her handsome son. Chains dropped his family off here before he left.

The sacrifices my family has been making to help me get my woman back warms my heart are many.

I'll never be able to repay them.

CHAPTER TWENTY-FIVE
Rachel

I haven't been able to move around for a few days now. Each night, as promised, Mike comes into my cell and whips my back.

I got a look at what he's been beating me with the other day. The handle was just a little bigger than Mike's hand, brown, smooth, and looked like wood. Protruding from the handle are long thin bits of brown leather.

I remember Mike laughing when he saw my face. He told me that it was his *siete rayas amigo,* which he translated for me to mean Seven stripped friend.

Every night, after my ten strikes, Carlos comes back and asks me the same question.

"Do you accept me of your own free will?"

Is this what he thinks of as free will? This is coercion control. He has people beaten until they give him what he wants just to have the beatings stopped. But I haven't told him that. Actually, I haven't said a single word since that first day.

Mike lands strike ten on my back and I scream at the pain it causes. By the time I'm able to get myself under control, Mike has already left my cell.

I hear Carlos clear his throat.

I decide to break my silence and answer Carlos's question today. Using every single bit of strength I have, which isn't much, I manage to roll over onto my side and sit up.

I don't have enough strength to do anything more. My legs are laying crossed because I just can't find it in me to bend forward and uncross them.

"Have you finally decided to accept me of your own free will?" He asks.

I try and fight back the chills running through my body. I'm freezing. Probably because it's cold in here and I haven't had a shirt on since Mike ripped mine off the very first day.

I reach up to wipe my brow as sweat drops into my eyes.

Wait! How can I be sweating if I'm so freaking cold?

"Well," Carlos says impatiently. His voice seems far away but I chalk it to the echo in this room of empty cells.

"Fu..ck yyy...oouu!"

There. He has my answer. Now I can rest up and regain enough strength for tomorrows beating.

I start falling backwards but am out before I land on my back.

Carlos

Estúpida. Stupid girl. Why won't she just give in? I do love her spirit though. She will make for a fine wife. My son was an idiot. The boy deserved to die for landing his father in jail.

I made his life simple. I even procured his wife when she was but an infant. And he fucked the whole thing up.

Estúpido.

However, his last sacrifice before he died has earned him back in my favor. He repaid the price and brought me the perfect wife. Even if he didn't fully know it. The moment I saw pretty girl Rachel I thought she was the most beautiful woman I had ever seen.

Then I witnessed her sass. It made me smile.

But the icing on the cake was her plan to kill Roman using the gas from his fireplace.

Absolutely brilliant.

She had to be mine. So, I made it so.

I'm standing outside of her cell watching her sleep, but something seems off. Unlocking her cell, I walk to her side.

She doesn't look like she's sleeping. She looks dead. Her face is pale and a thin layer of sweat covers her skin.

I roll her over and look at her back. I expected the marks, even craved to see them. But I didn't expect this.

A few of the cuts on the bottom of her back are infected.

"Mike," I yell. "Get me the medkit and call Doctor Andrews. We need to take her in first thing in the morning for antibiotics."

Mike does as I ask, and I get to work cleaning her back. Andrews knows to keep his mouth shut about everything he sees. We don't allow him inside the compound so we're going to have to take her to him.

I will allow her a little time to heal before subjecting her to Mike again. It might take time, but she will submit.

CHAPTER TWENTY-SIX
Ink

"They're pulling in now," I say into the radio. "I can't tell how many are inside because the windows are tented."

"Is there only one vehicle?" Wolf's voice comes through my earpiece.

"Affirmative. The suspect has no escorts. We can take it from here on our end. Stay safe. Over and out."

I look over at Slim and grin. He's having way too much fun.

"Affirmative?" I ask.

"What?" he says, innocently. "I feel like a spy and I'm loving it. You're just jealous because I'm dressed for success and you're wearing jeans and a white t-shirt."

I look down at Slim's outfit. He's wearing all black. Skintight leggings and a tight long-sleeved turtleneck.

"Alright," I admit. "You are dressed for the part."

Slim smiles.

"Almost," I finish. "What's up with the high-heeled boots and cat ears?"

Hawk chuckles from somewhere behind us.

"If it comes down to it and we have to run, you're screwed," I tell him.

Slim stands from our crouched position. He stands tall

and firm.

"If someone started chasing us, I would still outrun you all in these heels," he says confidently. "And I would look fucking awesome doing it. Not to mention I could use my heels as a very effective weapon."

"Your man is one scary human," Wolf says over the radio. "Also, you forgot to put yourselves on mute."

Slim blushes which causes both me and Hawk to laugh.

When the radios are muted on our end, we sit silently and wait for Wolf to make his move. His earpiece is set for open communication. Which means we can hear everything anyone near him says.

"Who the hell are you?" We hear.

"Hola, mi nombre es Lobo. Soy el asistente del Dr. Andrews. Depe ser el Sr. Hernández."

"Wolf speaks Spanish?" I ask, shocked. "What the hell did he say?"

"He said that his name was Wolf and that he was the doctor's assistant."

"You speak Spanish?" I ask, equally as shocked.

"Some of us paid attention in school," Slim teases.

"Do you speak English, *hombre*?"

"I do," Wolf answers. "I'm sorry, I just heard you talking to your female in Spanish and I assumed it would be easier for you if I did as well."

We hear a deep chuckle. "I see," the man says. "Well, to answer your question, yes, I am Carlos Hernández. You're new. How long have you been here?"

"I'm only here until the doctor's regular assistant returns. He had an appointment and asked me to fill in for the day."

"I see. Well, we have an appointment to see Dr. Andrews."

"Of course, Mr. Hernández. If you would just follow me to a waiting room. Would you like a wheelchair for Mrs. Hernández?"

I burn with anger at not only hearing Wolf call her Mrs. Hernández, but with the fact that my woman is so close, and I can't touch or see her.

"No thank you. And call me Carlos."

"Of course, Carlos."

"Just lay her on the bed and the doctor will be in with you shortly."

A few minutes go by before Wolf speaks.

"She's in the room and awake," he tells us. "She looks rough, brother, I'm not going to lie. But she's alive."

"Did she recognize you?" I ask, desperate for any information.

"Are they here?" Someone asks on Wolf's end.

"They're in room seven," Wolf answers.

"Thank you, Wolf. I might need your help with her. I'm not sure if she's going to need to be sedated or not. Just keep a listen for me."

"Of course."

We wait.

"You need to take some deep breaths, brother," Hawk says. "Keep your mind clear."

He's right, of course. I'm a second away from kicking down the door and killing any fucker between me and my woman.

"She did," Wolf finally says. "She's hurt, I can tell from her eyes, but she smiled."

That's my girl. Tough as nails and stubborn to no end.

Wolf had to sign a paper when he was 'hired'. It stated that he wasn't allowed to speak about anything he sees, hears, or learns while working there.

Slim assures us, legally standing, that he should be fine. Wolf didn't sign his legal name so it shouldn't hold in court.

We're hoping so anyway.

"Wolf, please join me," we hear Dr. Andrews say.

"Next time something like this happens," Slim says, clearly frustrated. "The person going it is wearing glasses with a built-in camera."

"Hopefully, there will never be a next time," Hawk says.

"Remember what you signed?" the doctor asks.

"Yes, sir," Wolf answers. "Nothing leaves this room."

"Mrs. Hernández has some marks made from a whip across her back. A few have become infected and we need to treat her with a series of antibiotic shots as well as a steroid shot."

I don't realize doing it, but I must have started running towards the building. Hawk tackles me to the ground and holds me there until I get myself under control.

"If she decides she needs out now, then we'll get her out," Hawk says. "But if you run in there now, you're liable to get a lot of people killed."

Damnit.

"I need you to clean her back and bandage it up," the doctor's voice echoes in my ear. "I'll go get the injections prepared."

"You know the rules, doc," Carlos speaks up. "I monitor every injection you give."

"Of course," doc sighs.

"As for you," Carlos continues. "I have someone on the other side of this door. Do not leave this room until I return."

"Yes, Mr. Hernández," Wolf says calmly.

We hear the door open and close, but the room stays silent.

I fall to the ground next to Slim and wait.

"Wolf."

I'm thrown back by the sound of Rachel's voice. I'm overjoyed to hear it and know that she's still alive. But she sounds tired. Almost, too tired.

"What are you doing here?" she asks. "Is Sammy okay?"

"Ink is fine," Wolf says quietly. "He can hear everything you say. Along with the rest of the team. As to what I'm doing here, well that's up to you."

"What do you mean?" she asks.

"Let's get started on this back first," Wolf tells her. "I'm going to give you a shot to numb the area. Small pinch."

We hear Rachel inhale a quick breath.

"There, it won't take long to kick in."

"What's going on?" Rachel asks.

"Tell me what happened to your back first," he says.

Slim unmutes our side before speaking.

"Wolf, as much as we all want to know what she's been through, we don't have time."

"I've been told our time is short," Wolf says. "Here's the plan. You have two choices. I can either get you out of here now. Which wouldn't be easy, and we could both be killed. Or you could go back inside the compound and help us find a way inside. We could get you out safely within a few days and take down the entire Hernández Cartel."

"That's not much of a choice," I hear Rachel say. "As you can tell from my back, my time hasn't been fun. If I go back inside, there's no way for me to help you. My room is a locked prison cell. Not to mention that I've been too weak to even move around in bed, let alone push myself around in that child's wheelchair that they gave me."

"We have these," Wolf says. "It's very small and can easily fit inside your ear without being detected. You'll be able to hear us and we will be able to hear you."

"Alright," Rachel sighs. "But that still leaves... Ouch, I thought you numbed it?"

"Sorry, Miss Rachel, I'll give you another injection. There's a nasty slash that wraps around your left side. It's also infected."

"How bad does it look back there?" she asks.

"With antibiotics, you will heal up nicely. There will be scars though."

"I don't care about those," Rachel says. "Anyway, there's still the very real fact that I'm a prisoner."

"That's it," I say, standing. "I'm getting her out of there now."

"Ink, sit down and shut the fuck up."

Bear walks up and places his hand on my shoulder.

"Your woman is strong," he says. "Now let her strength outshine us all."

I sit back down with a resigned sigh. When I get my woman back, we're taking a nice long vacation. Just the two of us.

"Wolf," I whisper. "Tell her that I love her and that I'm so fucking proud of how strong she is."

"Don't you worry about it," Wolf tells Rachel. "I have an idea. I also have a message. Ink says that he is proud of you for being so strong and that he loves you."

I hear a snuffle and I know that Rachel's crying.
"I love you, too, Sammy," She whispers so softly that I almost missed it. "Yesterday before I passed out from the fever, I saw Mike bring in a group of girls. Girls, Sammy. They weren't women they were girls. The oldest is prob-

ably sixteen. And the youngest I saw had to be Sophia's age. She had to be at least two. I want to go back in. I'll do whatever it takes to help bring this damn family down for good."

The amount of pride and fear that rush through my body is intense.

"Who's Mike?" Wolf asks the question on all of our minds.

"I guess you could say he's Carlos's handyman."

"Who did this to your back?"

Now that's a question I want to know the answer to.

"It was Mike," she whispers. "Carlos has this insane idea that I am his queen to the Hernández empire. He wants me to submit to him of my own free will. I refuse daily and this is my punishment."

The room is quiet while Wolf works on her back.

"I went ahead and activated the earpiece," Slim says to Wolf. "Go ahead and slide it in her ear."

"I'm going to put this pretty deep in your ear," we hear Wolf say. "It won't hurt but it does feel weird."

A few seconds later, I hear her voice clearly as if she were in the room next to me.

"Can you hear me, Sammy?"

"I'm here, baby," I say, my eyes pooling over. "I'm so fucking sorry. I'll never forgive myself for letting you get taken."

"It's not your fault," she says, clearly emotional. "It was mine and I did it because he had my sister. Did she ever show up?"

She did, not long after we discovered Rachel was missing. I tell her as much.

"Listen," she says. "I need to go back inside. I need you guys to help those little girls. Will I be able to hear you from inside the building?"

"You will, honey," Slim answers. "I made these myself and am confident in their range."

"Alright, then I need to do this."

"They're coming," Wolf whispers urgently.

"We're going on mute, baby," I say quickly. "We can still everything you can, but you won't be able to hear us."

"I love you, Sammy," she whispers.

"Stay strong for me, Rachel."

I nod and Slim mutes our connection.

"Everything seems to be in order," we hear the doctor say. "Nice work Mr. Wolf."

"Thank you, Dr. Andrews," Wolf says, his voice calm. "I had to numb her back in order to clean out the dead tissue."

"Alright. Mrs. Hernández, I'm going to give you these shots to give the antibiotics and steroids a good start," the doctor says. "I've already given your husband the prescription. If all goes well, you should be feeling better within a few days."

"Thank you, Doctor," Carlos says. "I'll call you if anything changes."

"I do recommend not sleeping on your back, Mrs. Hernández," Wolf says. "It would only slow healing down."

"He's right, of course. You need plenty of rest and good food. I don't want you up and moving around until the infection is gone."

"Everything is taken care of, *mi Reina*. Let us go home."

"What the fuck does *mi Reina* mean?" Hawk asks.

"It means my queen," Slim answers. "He's obsessed with her."

"So am I," I growl. "And an obsessed man is a dangerous one. Especially if it's someone you love."

Hawk nods in agreement.

"I'm going to connect with Rachel," Slim says. "Be extremely quiet. I'm confident that no one will hear anything from her earpiece, but I don't want to take any chances."

It's always a good idea to listen to Slim.

"Rachel," Slim whispers. "Don't say anything and don't react. We are going to lose connection until you get back inside of the compound. I already have a signal booster in place for when we get there, but it won't work until we're in range. When we get to our location, I'll let you know we're there and you only respond when you're confident that no one can hear you."

"I love you, baby," I whisper. "Stay strong for me. We're going to end this shit fast."

Slim cuts off the signal and we race to our vehicle. I want to be in position before she gets back.

I can't fucking wait to wrap my hands around Carlos Hernández's neck. Or better yet, Mike.

CHAPTER TWENTY-SEVEN
Rachel

"You did well, *mi Reina*," Carlos says. "I was very impressed."

I'm sitting in the backseat of that same damn futuristic car that I freaking hate. Carlos is driving and Mike is in the passenger seat.

"One," I say with a new bout of courage. "I'm not your queen and of course I stayed quiet. Mike threatened to beat that five-year-old girl the same way he does me if I said a word."

Carlos laughs.

"He wouldn't have done it," he tells me. "Those girls are to be put up for auction. We can't have them parading around the stage with bumps and bruises on their precious little exposed bodies. It would lower their prices."

How is it possible for me to hate someone as much as I do this man?

I decide to keep quiet. I carefully lean back against the seat. The numbing shot that Wolf gave me hasn't worn off yet.

The corner of my lips twitch with the urge to smile but I hold it back.

Wolf was there. Sammy was nearby.

As much as I wanted to take Wolf up on his offer to get me out now, all I could think about was the parade of little girls I saw being locked in the cells around mine this morning.

I'll do whatever it takes to get them free.

"I've decided to let you stay in one of my rooms until you heal," Carlos says. "You can get a taste of the life I would give you. When your back is healed, I will give you the chance to change your answer. If not, then I'll put you back in the cell until you do. Mike is all for helping you pick the right answer."

"I'm sure he is," I mumble.

Carlos and Mike laugh as we make our way through the streets and back to the prison.

I sure hope Sammy and the guys know what they're about to walk into.

Ink

"We are not waiting another week," I roared. "There's no way in hell that Rachel can endure more beatings."

Wolf told me that Rachel's back didn't look good, but he wouldn't go into any further detail.

"I don't think that will happen until she's out of the water, Ink," Slim added. "From the sounds of it, Rachel is important to Carlos. He won't purposefully have her killed and any further beatings would do just that."

"She's important to me, Slim," I seethed. "She's the very beat of my heart and I will not have her locked inside that prison for another week."

"Alright," Slim sighed. "Then we'll have to work hard and smart to figure things out. Because if we aren't taking our time, then we need to be diligent about our moves."

"Have they arrived yet?" Wolf pants.

"Did you run all the way here?" Bear asks.

"No, not the whole way," Wolf answers. "I parked my

bike half a mile back and ran the rest of the way. Didn't want to take any chances on one of the guards hearing me."

"They're in the building," Trigger says through our earpieces. He and Brick are stationed on the other side of the building with another one of Slim's signal boosters in place. We aren't taking any chances of Rachel not being able to get through to us.

"Okay," Slim exclaims. "I'm going to go ahead and connect with Rachel. Everyone, stay silent."

"Rachel," Slim whispers. "We're here. If you can hear us, give me some sort of signal."

I sit silently as I wait to hear Rachel. A minute goes by and we hear nothing.

"Give her time," Slim says. "I can hear sound on her end, but no one is saying anything."

Finally, after another minute passes, we hear her.

"You know, Mike, just because Carlos says to jump off of a cliff doesn't mean you have to do it."

My anxiety spikes and calms at the same time. Hearing her voice is a balm on my soul that I didn't know I needed. However, learning that she's alone with Mike has me ready to break down the doors.

"I happen to like heights," Mike states.

"Heights, sure, but the landing is just going to get you killed."

"And who's going to do that?" Mike sneers. "Those bikers?"

"Those bikers are more man than you'll be."

"Speak your mind all you like, woman" he spat. "Just know that our visitations will come again soon, and this time, I won't be so gentle."

We hear a door slam shut and Rachel takes a deep

breath.

"Can you guys hear me?" she whispers.

"We're here," I say. "We're really close by, baby."

"Sammy," she cries. "These are horrible people."

"I know, baby," I soothe. "We're getting you out of there as fast as we can."

"No," she blurts. "Sammy, you have to get these kids out first. He plans to auction them off. He's going to make them parade around on a stage naked in front of a bunch of perverts. Promise me that you'll free them before coming after me."

I hate what she's asking me to do. She always comes first in my life. But then I think about those innocent children and there's only one response.

"Promise me, Sammy," she demands.

"I promise, sweetheart."

"Alright," Chains says. "If we're going to do this then we need to start planning. Rachel, honey, are you locked up?"

"No," she responds. "They've put me in a regular room on the second floor. I don't think they locked the door. They don't really view me as a threat."

"Are there any cameras?" Slim asks.

"I've been looking," she admits. "But I can't see any. Just as a precaution, I'm keeping my voice down and a blanket over my head."

I smile.

"Smart move," Trigger says. "I don't see very much security from my angle. Ink, how are things on your end."

"Same," I answer. "It looks dead."

"That's because they're all inside," Rachel tells us. "I don't know what's happening, but they're planning for some big event. Most likely the one involving the selling of these little girls."

"As much as I hate to admit it," Bear says. "We might have to call in the feds."

"Someone's coming," Rachel whispers urgently.

Not even a few seconds later, we hear her door open.

CHAPTER TWENTY-EIGHT
Rachel

"Are you enjoying your new room?" Carlos asks as he closes the door.

"I would be lying if I said no," I admit. "However, I would much prefer to be back in my cell. That way I have the constant reminder of how much of a dick you are."

Carlos laughs.

"I could arrange that if you want," he offers.

"Rachel, what the fuck are you doing?" Sammy whispers in my ear.

"Actually, I have a favor to ask," I say.

For some odd reason, Carlos has me in his future plans. Maybe I can play with that. He obviously craves my submission. Maybe I should give it to him.

His eyes widen as he sits on the side of the bed. This room is, by far, much better than the cell. The bed is nice and comfortable along with the rest of the room. But I need to remember what type of human this man is.

"As long as you obey, I'll give you anything, *mi Reina*," he tells me.

"Anything?" I ask.

"Well, almost anything," he chuckles.

"I want to go outside before the pain meds wear off," I say. "I just want to sit in the sunshine for a little while."

Carlos looks at me as he considers my request.

"Alright," he finally agrees. "But only for a few minutes. I have a ton of work to do to prepare for a party."

I want to ask what party he's talking about, but I honestly don't want to know the detail.

"I'm going to go grab your chair," he says before leaving.

"Rachel, what are you doing?" Sammy asks again.

I grab the blanket and easily toss it over my head. The numbing shot I received is starting to wear off and I can feel the tearing of my skin again.

"Carlos has carried me into this building twice now," I start. "And each time he's entered a code before the door unlocked to allow us is."

"Brilliant fucking woman." It takes me a second to recognize Trigger's voice. "You get us that code and we'll have our way inside."

"I'll be down in about half an hour," Carlos says from the other side of the door. "Get everything ready."

I pull my blanket back down and wait.

"People are so impatient," Carlos says when he opens the door. "Alright. Let's get you in this chair and out to some fresh air."

I have to hide my disgust for the man as he lifts me and places me in the child-sized wheelchair. The chair is too small, and the armrests are digging into my side.

But I don't complain.

"Remember," Carlos starts. "We can't stay outside for very long. But, if you continue to behave, I'll take you outside again tomorrow."

I nod my head.

Carlos pushes me down a long hallway and to an elevator that I don't remember seeing on the way up to the room.

We go inside and he presses the down button.

"I like this side of you," Carlos claims. "I think you might be coming around."

I'll let him think whatever he wants.

We make our way to the room where all the prison cells are and I want to scream as I see the little girls huddled close to each other behind one of the bars.

Carlos acts like nothing is wrong as he pushes me towards the door. He whistles a happy tune as he reaches for the keypad.

Seven...nine...four.

Crap I can't see the rest, his body was in the way.

When he opens the door, I push my way past and outside.

"The view isn't all that great here," Carlos admits as we stop a few feet outside the door. "It's a much more peaceful place at my family home. Unfortunately, I don't think we'll be able to go back."

I nod but keep my mouth shut. Anything he says, I want Sammy and the others to hear.

"Once everything is settled here, we'll travel to another home I own."

"See if you can get him to say more, Miss Rachel," Wolf says in my ear.

"Where is your other home?" I ask.

Carlos turns around and smiles. "I want it to be a surprise," he tells me. "But I truly think you'll love it. I've noticed that you feel uncomfortable around high-priced things. Our home is nothing fancy. Something simple and under the radar."

"Is it nearby?" I ask. "Will I be able to see my sister?"

"It's not too far," Carlos admits. "But we'll talk more about you seeing your sister a little further down the line."

I nod. Fuck face.

"Good job, baby," Sammy whispers. "You're doing great."

"We need to head back in, *mi Reina*. People are waiting for me."

Carlos walks towards the door and I quickly turn and angle myself.

Seven. Nine. Four.

I lean over and focus on his hands.

Seven, nine, four, eight, three, two, nine.

The door unlocks.

I want to smile and shout to the world, but I turn my head and look towards the sky.

Seven, nine, four, eight, three, two, nine.

Don't freaking forget, Rachel.

Seven, nine, four, eight, three, two, nine.

"*Mi Reina*, did you hear me?"

"I'm sorry. I was dazing," I lie. "What did you say."

"I asked if you were hungry?"

"You know, if you weren't such a monster, you'd actually be a good person."

Seven, nine, four, eight, three, two, nine.

Carlos laughs.

"You're probably right, *mi Reina*. But what would be the fun in that?"

Seven, nine, four, eight, three, two, nine.

Seven, nine, four, eight, three, two, nine.

I'm so focused on remembering the code that I space out. Before I know it, we're outside of the room.

"I'll have some food and your medication brought up to you," Carlos tells me. "I'll see you tomorrow."

He leaves and I'm left sitting in the child-sized wheelchair next to the bed. I don't want to talk for fear that there is a camera in here and they see my lips moving.

I lean my head back and cover my face with my hands. Trying to act frustrated.

"Seven, nine, four, eight, three, two, nine," I say quickly and quietly. "I can't talk. I'm still in my chair. The pain is coming back, and I don't think I can pull myself onto the bed."

"You did fucking great, baby," Sammy says. "Really fast, say the numbers one more time."

"Seven, nine, four, eight, three, two, nine," I respond.

The door flies open, and Carlos walks back inside.

"I forgot to put you back in bed," he says. "Sorry, *mi Reina*."

Carlos lifts me and flops me down on the bed. The pain that shoots through my back is unexpected and I scream.

Ink

Her scream makes me lose control.

"Ink, control yourself," I hear Wolf say. "Just listen."

"I'm okay," I hear Rachel say through the thunder in my ears. "Sammy, I'm okay. I just landed on my back wrong. It was mostly shock."

I calm down and listen to her voice.

"I need to get you out," I respond desperately. "Please, let me get you out of there."

"Sammy, listen," she whispers. "Just hold on for a little longer. We have to get these girls out of here before Carlos sells them to grown men for who knows what reasons. Stay strong for me, Sammy."

I'm taken aback by her words. She repeated the same thing I said. Stay strong for me.

"Slim," I say. "Any luck yet?"

Slim has been working fast to access any security cameras that might be inside the compound. As soon as we have that access, we can work on getting inside.

"I think so big guy," he tells me. "We should talk about what Bear said."

"About calling the feds?" I ask.

"Yeah," Slim responds. "I think it's a good idea."

"Especially considering there are children inside," Trigger says. "I'll kill every mother fucker in there if I find out they are hurting children."

"And you think the police force will be able to stop you?" I hear Brick ask. "I'll be holding those fuckers back while you bathe in the blood of everyone inside that building."

"Kinky," Rachel whispers.

"Bingo," Slim celebrates. "I'm in and hiding behind a firewall. No one will be able to find me."

"I thought firewalls prevented people from accessing their systems?" Rachel asks.

Her voice sounds rough and I know that she's in more pain than she's letting on.

"You're absolutely correct, honey," Slim says. "But I've found a way to use it to my advantage. Now, I have access to their entire system and they'll never even know that I'm in."

"Remind me not to make you mad," she mumbled, causing Slim, Hawk, and Wolf to laugh.

"What have you got?" Bear asks.

"Well," Slim starts. "I can't see Rachel anywhere. So, it's safe to say that there isn't a camera in her room."

"Are you sure?" I ask.

Slim looks at me with raised brows.

"You're safe to speak without that blanket on your

head," I tell Rachel, causing Slim to chuckle. "Just keep as quiet as you can."

"Oh God," Slim exclaims. "It's worse than we thought."

I walk over and glance down at Slim's laptop. The images popping up on his screen make my stomach sour.

Children, both boys, and girls of all ages are in multiple cells throughout the building.

"They're naked, Hawk," Slim whispers, tears falling down his face. "They're all naked and scared."

Hawk wraps Slim in his arms.

"We'll get them out, sweet boy," Hawk soothes. "We'll get them all out and back to their families."

"Do you see them, Sammy?" Rachel asks. "Do you see those little kids? Please, save them."

"Yeah," I whisper back. "I see them, baby. We're going to get you all out."

◆ ◆ ◆

It takes over an hour, but we finally come up with a plan.

It won't be much longer, and those kids will be free, and I'll have my woman in my arms. Where she will stay for the rest of her life.

"I can help, guys," Rachel says. She's been listening in on the plan and has kept quiet until now.

"There's an elevator that can take me down to the lower floor. I watched Mike place the cell keys in the exact same spot for two weeks straight

. I can get the kids in this part of the building out while you work on the rest."

"Absolutely fucking not," I growl. "You stay right where you are until I come and get you."

Slim looks at me with wide eyes.

"*Idiot,*" he mouths silently.

"I'll have you know that I am not a freaking child, Sam," Rachel seethes.

"She's about to blow," Slim laughs.

"I don't need your permission to do a damn thing," Rachel continues, her voice rising. "I'm going down to the lower level and I am going to release those kids and there isn't a damn thing you can do to stop me."

"Miss Rachel," Wolf speaks up. "You really need to lower your voice before someone hears. Yell at Ink softly, please."

A few seconds pause and Rachel starts giggling.

"Sorry guys," she whispers. "But I am doing it, Sammy."

"It's not that I think you're incapable, baby," I tell her. "If you release those kids too early then they could get hurt or used as hostages. Or even yourself."

"I have a plan," she admits. "There's only one key to those cells. Mike misplaced it once and he and Carlos had an all-out war about his incompetence. So, Mike always places the key in the same spot every single time he locks a cell door."

"What's your plan?" Brick's voice echoes through my earpiece.

"If I can get down a few minutes before you burst in, I can unlock the cell door and enter into the cage with the kids. And the key."

I have to admit it's not a bad plan. She would be safer inside a locked room than one where anyone can enter.

"They could still shoot you," Trigger reminds us.

"Maybe," Rachel admits. "But it would be better than being used as a sex slave for the rest of our lives."

"If everything goes as planned, then what she's suggesting would be the best choice," I tell the group. "The second we make our move Carlos will know who it is. The first thing he's going to do is go straight to Rachel and use her as leverage to get away."

"Just let me know a few minutes before," Rachel says. "That's all I need."

"What about your back?" Bear asks. "Will you be able to handle moving yourself around fast enough to get the job done quickly?"

"Don't you worry about me," Rachel assures us. "You just worry about getting your asses in here fast enough. And don't get yourselves killed."

Yes, ma'am, sounds out and we sit back and wait for the chance to strike.

CHAPTER TWENTY-NINE
Rachel

What in the world has my life become?

As strange as it sounds, I'm pumped up on adrenaline and all fear has washed from my body. I think it's because I know Sammy is nearby. The moment I heard his voice for the first time in two weeks, I felt immensely stronger.

A knock on my door startles me and I hear the voices through the earpiece telling each other to hush.

"Yes?" I answer.

A woman opens the door and walks in holding a tray.

"I thought I was the only adult female here," I admit.

The woman chuckles.

"Most days, you are," she says. "I only come when the cleaning services come. Can't let them wander around on their own. I'm Carlos` sister, Elizabeth."

I take the tray she offers and sit it beside me on the bed.

"Do you have any idea that kind of horrible things they do here?" I ask her, trying to keep the contempt out of my voice.

"Easy, baby," Sammy says in my ear.

"I am aware," she admits, lowering her voice. "I've tried helping others out of here before and it landed me with a broken arm and a dead son. If you were in my shoes, what would you do?"

"I'm sorry about your son," I say, surprised that she's even attempted to help someone. "But think about all the other families, the mothers, who lose their children to people like your brother."

"I don't have a choice," she seethes. "He's already taken my only child away and all I have left is my own life."

"We always have a choice," I tell her. "It's not always the easiest choice, and sometimes it may not always be the best one, but there is always a choice. And honestly, I would rather he take my life than for me sit by like a coward and let him sell little kids to rapists."

"Damnit Rachel," Sammy yells. "You're telling her too much."

He's probably right, but I have a gut feeling about this woman. She's probably in her late forties or early fifties but her eyes look like they've lived many lifetimes.

She's exhausted and I just know that she has a good heart.

"I love my brother," she admits softly. "But he's not a good man. His son wasn't a good man. And there are days when I'm glad he took my son's life because he was growing to be just as mean and hateful."

She sits on my bed with her head hung low.

"Why are you telling me these things?" I ask.

Elizabeth looks up and gifts me with a sad smile.

"Because you remind me of myself at your age. Stubborn, hardheaded, and full of defiance. Please, don't lose that part of you, don't let my brother take who you are and mold you into who I am."

I nod but remain silent.

"Are you in love, Rachel?" she asks.

The thought of Sammy makes me smile.

"I am," I admit.

"Good," she says, standing. "Love is a good thing. It's a strong thing. Love is a bond that no man can break."

Elizabeth walks to the door. With her hand on the doorknob, she turns and looks at me one last time, tears streaming down her face.

"My brother and all his staff and guests have a get-together planned in the next hour. It will be in the basement. There is only one way out. The door will be locked from the inside and I am the only one with the key."

"Why are you telling me this?" I whisper, shocked at what she's saying.

"My brother has to pay for the crimes he's committed," She whispers. "You were right, we always a choice. And this is mine. Be careful Rachel, Mike never attends those meetings."

"Thank you, Elizabeth," I say, not holding back my tears.

"Tell the man you love to hold you tight when he comes to save you," she says, a soft smile on her lips. "Tell him not to worry about Carlos. I'll take care of my brother the way he deserves."

Without another word, she opens the door and leaves.

"What just happened?" I whisper.

"I think Carlos's sister just gave us the in that we need," Wolf says.

"Trigger, Hawk, come over and join us."

"On it, prez."

"Get ready, baby," Sammy tells me. "I need you focused on your part. Get down there and locked into that cell with those girls. Got it?"

"I'm already halfway on the chair," I grunt, ignoring the pain in my back.

What does Elizabeth have planned?

Elizabeth

There comes a time in a woman's life when she has to put her foot down. Well, that time passed a long time ago. I have watched for years as my brothers and nephews killed, stole, lied, corrupted, and schemed their way to where they are today.

I watched as this new batch of children were led inside and locked away. I watched from the security monitor as Mike beat the pretty handicapped woman while my brother stood to the side, watching.

I think that's what finally broke me. Not when he killed his own son. Hell, not when he killed mine. Or our parents, for that matter. But when I saw how resilient and strong this woman was.

That's how I used to be. There was no way I'm going to let him break down another woman. No way I'm going to let him sell another child.

Visiting Rachel was what I needed to get the courage to do what needs to be done.

My brother has these special meetings once a month. Everyone will go to the basement for drinks and to discuss prices for whatever Carlos is currently selling. My job is to keep the door locked, with the only key, and not to unlock until one of my brothers gives me the okay.

I wait until every last member of this wretched place that are here today, and every guest is inside. I step in, lock the two locks, and secure the deadbolts. Then with my back turned, I place the key in my mouth and swallow.

In five minutes' time, the air conditioner will turn on and release a tasteless and odorless gas into the air. Within minutes, every single soul in this room will be dead.

This has been my plan for years. I only wished I had done it sooner.

Turning around, I sit down on the steps in front of the door and listen to the men laugh and drink. I close my eyes and think of Rachel. I can only pray that she makes it out of here before Mike gets his hands on her.

Get out, woman! Save those babies. Save yourself.

The air kicks on and I smile.

CHAPTER THIRTY
Ink

"It's been an hour," Rachel's sweet voice says in my ear.

"I haven't seen movement in a while," Chains tells us.

"Let's get this party started," Trigger says, already waltzing forward.

"Damnit, Trigger, wait for the rest of us," Brick grumps, running after him.

"Go now, baby," I say. "And, please, be careful."

"On my way," her sweet voice says in my ear. "Going silent."

I hate what she's about to do. If we can trust this Elizabeth chick, then Carlos and most of the people inside that building will be trapped. But Rachel still has to watch out for fucking Mike or random people.

"Ready, brother?" Wolf asks.

"More than," I admit.

It takes us five minutes to reach the gate. By the time I get there, Trigger and Brick have already taken care of the guards and have the gate opened.

"You work fast," Chains exclaims.

"They were cowards," Trigger grumps.

Brick just laughs. "Trig wanted a fight and they bent like twigs."

"I'm in," Rachel whispers. "We're in the fifth cell and we're all hiding in the back."

"Rachel, is there a bed in the cell with you?" Bear asks.

"Yeah," she answers.

"Good, grab the mattress and place it in front of you. It's not much but it will give you and the kids the best protection until we can get you out safely."

We hear Rachel talking to the little girls. Trying to get them calm.

"Here, sweetie," she says. "Take my shirt. I want all of you to get behind my chair and try to stay as quiet as you can. Oh crap, Sammy I have a problem."

"What?" I ask frantically.

"I don't think any of these kids speak English. Espanol?"

"Si," a little girl answers.

"I got this, guys," Slim says in our ears. "Rachel, just repeat after me. I'll say the exact same thing you just asked them to do."

"Alright, brothers, let's go."

Rachel

I watch as the door opens, and the guys walk in. I have never in my life felt so much relief.

"Baby," I hear Sammy whisper. Except this time, not only can I hear it in one of my ears, but up close and personal. I peer around the thin mattress and smile when I see his hands wrapped around the other side of the bars.

"I'm here," I whisper. I want so much to drop the mattress and dash to him as fast as possible. To feel his arms around me again. But I don't move.

"Almost, baby," he says as if he's reading my mind. "Almost."

"Don't move from this cell, Miss Rachel," Wolf tells me.

I smile at wolf. "I won't."

Sammy stands there for a second longer before following his men deeper into the building.

"Guys," Slim says through the earpiece. "Detective Dick is ten minutes out and he's pissed that you didn't wait."

I hear a couple of the guys snort, but they don't respond.

"You doing okay, Rachel?" Slim asks.

"Yeah, we are," I whisper.

Suddenly I hear a deep guttural grunt and a loud thud through my ears.

"Rachel, sweetheart," I hear Brick say. "Have you met a large beefy man with a face full of scars?"

"That sounds like Mike," I say.

"Don't fucking touch him" Sammy orders. "He's mine."

"I'll tie him up and toss him in this here closet," Brick says cheerfully. "We'll collect him on the way out."

I shake my head and smile. I might not be able to exact my revenge against Frankie and Antonio, but it looks like Mike won't be getting so lucky.

I sit here for ten minutes as I listen to the men locate all the children. Luckily, they didn't run into very many of Carlos's men. The ones they did were "taken care of" by Trigger. I'm not sure if that means knocked out or killed. I'm also not sure that I care.

"Please tell me that there are no more, Slim," Chains begs. "My heart can't take much more."

"The last group is the ones with Rachel," He answers.

"Hey guys, I think I found the basement door," Bear says. "It's locked from the inside just like the woman said."

"It's quiet," Wolf says.

"Wrap it up, guys," Slim orders. "Our favorite detective just arrived."

"Let's get you out of here," Sammy says. I look up and see him back on the other side of the cell.

"Key's baby," he demands.

"Estas segura," I tell the girls. "You're safe."

Ignoring the burn in my back, I arch my arm and throw the iron key. The next thing I know, Sammy falls to his knees and puts his head in my lap.

"Sammy, I stink," I cry, just as happy that he's here. "I haven't had a shower since I've been here."

I rub my fingers through his short hair, loving the feeling of the heat coming off his body.

"You smell amazing," he says, standing. "You look amazing, you feel amazing and you taste amazing."

Sammy leans down and kisses me like I've never been kissed before.

He pulls back and looked me up and down.

"Let's get you home," he says. "Well, to a hospital first, then home."

The other men walk into the cell with some new men I've never seen before. They're all wearing suits and I can see their badges shining on the side of their pants. These must be the feds they were talking about.

"What the fuck was going on here?" One of them asks.

"These kids don't speak English," I say. "They're going to need a translator."

One of the men walks over and glances at Sammy before landing his eyes on me.

"I have some questions, ma`am," he says.

I'm about to speak when Sammy stops me.

"She's going to a hospital," he demands. "Your questions can come later."

He nods reluctantly.

"Can I pick you up?" Sammy asks.

Man, that sounds like the best idea I've ever heard. But I shake my head.

"As much as I would love that, I honestly don't think I could handle the pain," I admit.

His face is hard as he walks behind me and starts pushing the chair.

"Hey Sammy," I say. "I think I'm ready for that tattoo now."

Tilting my head back, I watch as the corner of his lips tilt up.

"When you're better, we'll talk about it," he says.

I close my eyes and relax as Sammy pushes me outside. I'm in a pair of leggings and a bra, having given my shirt to the youngest girl I met. They were all naked, but I couldn't clothe them all.

When we reach outside, I look up and bask in the sunlight. It looks like the day is almost over, but the sun isn't willing to let go of this side of the world just yet. The sky is dancing with beautiful waves of blues, oranges, and a bit of pink.

"Oh, god, baby," Sammy sighs. "Your back. You have to be in so much pain."

The next thing I know, I'm being placed stomach down on a gurney and shoved into an ambulance. Sammy right next to me.

"Don't forget to pick up that package," I hear Sammy say.

"Already taken care of," Brick answers through my ear.

Knowing that Sammy is here beside me, I gently dig in my ear and pull out the smallest listening device I have ever seen. It's been plugging my ear for hours now and it's nice to have full listening range in both ears again.

"Can I take a nap now?" I ask no one in particular.

Before anyone can answer, I close my eyes and sleep the deepest sleep I have slept in a very long time.

EPILOGUE
Ink

It's been two months since we rescued Rachel and those children from the Hernández compound. Detective Dick said he found thirty-seven men and one woman in the basement. All dead from Carbon monoxide poisoning.

Which was ironic, considering that's how Rachel tried killing herself and Roman and how Carlos inevitably did kill his son.

We gave the police the list of names that Slim found. We'll let them handle tracking the rest of those damn members down.

Except for three of them. Rachel told us an about location on where to find the men that held her down and raped her.

We have Mike, Antonio, and Frankie at an undisclosed location where they will slowly die the most painful and horrific death I can think of. I haven't thought of it just yet, I've had other things on my mind. But in the meantime, Trigger was more than happy to make sure they're not comfortable. He leaves that building daily with blood on his body and a smile on his face.

It could take me a really long time to think something up and I'm not sure Trigger minds that in the least.

All of the children were rescued and returned to their families. Slim found a list of previous children that the bastard sold. There were hundreds. I'm not sure what's happening with that, but we've been assured that the police are doing their best to track them all down.

As for Rachel, I've moved her into my home. I didn't ask but she doesn't seem to mind. I've spent the past month making sure she has everything she could need to live a life as comfortable as she wants.

Her back is finally healed but the doctor said it would most likely scar. She was scared at first of having so many scars, but I've assured her many times that I'm only reminded of her bravery and strength when I look at them.

Rose and Rachel talk about how they both have the same type of scars on their backs. I've even caught them comparing them. I hate that it's something they both went through but I'm glad that they're not afraid to talk about it.

Brave women.

Speaking of Rose, she has started going through In Vitro Fertilization. They're going to see if they can get Rose pregnant using Hawk's sperm. Bear isn't all that happy about it when people are looking, but the second he watches Slim and Hawk, you can see the pride and happiness in his face.

We are all hoping that Rose is able to get pregnant soon, though, because Bear is taking out his lack of sex on all of us. They want to make sure that if she gets pregnant, it's because of the fertilized egg with Hawk's sperm that was implanted and not one from Bear.

I walk into my room and stop when I see Rachel, butt ass naked, making her way from our bed to the floor.

"Baby," I say. "What are you doing?"

She stops moving and sighs.

"I dropped my charger cord again," she says, clearly aggravated.

"I rather like what's happening right now," I tease. "Your ass is up and begging me to take it."

"Don't you dare put your dick anywhere near my ass," she proclaims.

"It will happen," I assure her. "I will claim that ass just as I have claimed your mouth, your tits, and your pussy."

Rachel shakes her head and makes her way back onto the bed.

We've found fun and inventive ways for us to make love in multiple positions. I've even bought her a special pillow called a Liberator wedge. It's designed for disabled women to help with sexual positions.

I grab the pillow from the closet and make my way to the bed.

"Trying to say something?" she teases.

I just smile and place the wedge on the bed. I grab my woman and place her face down on top of the wedge. The pillow is designed to mimic doggy style, among others. It's our second favorite way to have sex.

Already knowing she's wet for me I reach down and slide my fingers through her juicy folds.

"I'm already so sensitive," she moans.

I smile. It won't take but a special touch to make her come.

I pull out my aching cock and stroke it a few times.

"I want a taste," she tells me.

Without a second thought, I crawl to the front of her and offer her the treat.

She wraps her amazing lips around my cock, and I moan as the feeling of her wet mouth engulfs me.

"So fucking good, baby," I praise.

Leaning down, I angle her head slightly back and shove my dick down further. The tip reaches her throat causing her to gag.

"Swallow, Rachel," I demand. "You wanted to taste, so fucking swallow my cock."

My beautiful woman, always so eager for more, swallows and my dick moves further down. I hold it there for a few seconds before pulling out.

Rachel takes a deep breath before grabbing my ass and shoving me back inside her mouth.

"Greedy girl," I chuckle.

But I don't mind. I fuck her mouth until I lose my patience.

"Don't fucking move," I growl. "There will be no gentle this time. I'm going to fuck you until I can't see straight. But first, I'm going to taste you."

Pulling her ass cheeks apart, I take a good look at the beautiful sight. Her small pucker pulsates. She says she doesn't want ass play, but her ass is telling me different. I dip my finger in her juices and rub gentle circles around her pucker.

"Sammy," she moans. "I'm not ready for that."

"I know, baby," I soothe. "My dick isn't going in here today, just my finger."

"Samm... oh, dear lord, don't stop," she moans.

I work my finger in and out and lean down to suck in her juices.

Best tasting snack I've ever had.

I finger fuck her ass faster as I delve into her pussy with no remorse. My tongue explores as if it's the first time he's ever tasted pussy. I dip into her tight hole before pulling her tiny clit into my mouth and flicking it back and forth.

"Sammy, I'm coming," she moans.

I add a second finger to her ass and lick that clit until her ass squeezes my fingers so hard that I can no longer move them.

"Good girl," I praise. "So very good."

I sit back up on my knees and shove my cock deep inside my woman.

"Oh God, yes," she screams. "I need you to fuck me hard, Sammy. Please."

"Never beg, baby," I tell her. "I'll always give you what you need."

I pull back and shove myself back inside. I'm slow and gentle as I enjoy the feeling of her tight pussy around my aching cock.

"Sammy," she complains.

I smile, then fuck her hard enough to rattle the headboard.

"God, yes," she moans. "I'm gonna come, Sammy."

I love when my woman comes while I'm just fucking her.

I feel her pussy squeeze down on my dick and I know she's seconds away from coming. I thrust relentlessly as I demand a release of my own.

Rachel screams, arches her back, and comes all over my dick. The feeling of her tight pussy growing even tighter triggers my release and I explode deep inside of her.

I fall forward against her back, my dick still balls deep in her pussy, and I just lay there.

"As much as I love you," I say after a minute or so. "I really have to piss."

Rachel laughs.

"Sammy," she giggles. "Shut the fuck up and kiss me."

I smile and do as the woman demands. I kiss her lips before kissing my way to the back of her shoulder where a small tattoo sits.

A simple bow arrow with the word 'warrior' written above it. Because that's what she is. A fucking warrior.

I'll forever be thankful to this warrior, this beautiful woman, for giving me a second chance.

THE END

Author's Note

Holy cow! Ink and Rachel put me through the wringer with this one. I wasn't sure if I was going to actually make it through it a few times. We did go a bit darker this time and it was tough to write, but I pulled through.

Let's talk Wolf. So many people have asked (demanded) for his story. I wasn't sure for the longest time, but I decided that I will give you Wolf. I didn't write an epilogue from his point of view in this book like I normally would because, frankly, I don't know his story yet. So, he and I are going to have a sit down here in a few days and get some things sorted.

Reviews are an author's best friend. It would mean a great deal to me if you would consider leaving a review on Amazon or Goodreads. Even just a few words would be amazing. I would absolutely love hearing what you have to say about Ink and Rachel's story.

I like to do random giveaways. Sometimes it's a signed book, or sometimes it could just be a bookmark. You never know with me. If you would like to enter to win one of these random giveaways or want to stay up to date on all future releases, join us at Carol's Infernal Riders.

You can also join my newsletter to get the same information. http://eepurl.com/gKAehT

I know not everyone has Facebook. If you would like to reach out and contact me, my email is

authorcaroldawn@outlook.com

Also, by Carol Dawn

Infernal Sons MC, Series
Bear's Forever
A Very Beary Christmas
Chains' Redemption
Hawk's Choice
Ma
Trigger's Light
Brick's Fight

Audible
Bear's Forever audio

ABOUT THE AUTHOR

Carol Dawn

Carol Dawn was born in Maysville, Kentucky, USA, under the name Carolyn Jacobs. Carol is a stay-at-home mom where she spends her days making pb&j sandwiches, picking up toys, and giving her kids more cuddles than they want.

At the young age of five, Carol received a reading medallion for reading over twenty-one books in an eight-week period. So, her literary journey began. She wrote poems, songs, short stories and read many books.

Carol has a slight (MASSIVE) obsession with alpha male/insta-love romance books. If she isn't reading about them, she's writing about them.

When she isn't writing, reading or playing mom, you will find her watching re-runs of Stargate SG1, Startrek, cooking, crafting, or performing her favorite songs for her invisible audience.

Printed in Great Britain
by Amazon